MW01108930

```
J           25.00      03/18
SUM    Day, Nick
       Surprised?
```

DATE DUE			

WITHDRAWN

Summer Road Trip

Surprised?

BY NICK DAY

EPIC Escape
An Imprint of EPIC Press
abdopublishing.com

Surprised?
Summer Road Trip

Written by Nick Day

Copyright © 2018 by Abdo Consulting Group, Inc.

Published by EPIC Press™
PO Box 398166
Minneapolis, MN 55439

Cover design by Christina Doffing
Images for cover art obtained from iStock
Edited by Rue Moran

LIBRARY OF CONGRESS CATALOGING-IN-PUBLICATION DATA
Names: Day, Nick, author.
Title: Surprised?/ by Nick Day
Description: Minneapolis, MN : EPIC Press, 2018 | Series: Summer road trip
Summary: Sara is nearing the end of her first year at college, and can't wait for summer
    vacation. But out of nowhere she gets a surprising phone call: her estranged father is getting
    remarried—and he wants her at the wedding. Sara's best friend Pete volunteers to drive to
    Texas with her. What follows is a summer Sara will never forget—for better or for worse.
Identifiers: LCCN 2016962618 | ISBN 9781680767261 (lib. bdg.)
    | ISBN 9781680767827 (ebook)
Subjects: LCSH: Adventure stories—Fiction. | Travel—Fiction. | Stepfamilies—Fiction.
    | Best friends—Fiction—Fiction | Young adult fiction.
Classification: DDC [FIC]—dc23
LC record available at http://lccn.loc.gov/2016962618

To my family

Chapter One

THE SUN WAS PEEKING OUT FROM BEHIND THE HIGH clouds as I pushed open the heavy wooden doors of Harris Hall. I had just finished my last final and my freshman year in college was officially behind me.

"Sara!" came a familiar bright voice from behind me. I turned to see Pete, smiley as ever, striding toward me. "Not bad, right?"

"Yeah, not too brutal! Except that last question," I said.

"Don't worry, nobody ever knows what E. E. Cummings poems mean," Pete said, laughing.

Pete was one of only three guys in our poetry class.

I was sure the only reason he enrolled was because he knew I'd be there. He claimed otherwise ("I just like learning about new things!") but I've always been a little skeptical of his intentions. Not that I really mind. He's one of my best friends, after all.

"So, whaddya wanna do to celebrate?" Pete asked me, stuffing his hands in the front pocket of his purple Northwestern Wildcats sweatshirt. Pete wears Wildcats stuff every single day, rain or shine.

"I dunno—maybe get something to eat that's not Allison Hall powdered eggs?"

"Oh, absolutely." Pete grinned at the idea. Though we'd been friends for an entire school year, I didn't think I'd ever seen him frown.

"Hey, nerds!" I spun around to see my roommate, Maria, bounding toward me. "Finally done? I've been waiting to hang out all week!" She was a theater major. They got off easy. "Let's do something fun, I have to leave for the airport in an hour!"

"What, already?" I gasped. "I thought you guys were leaving tomorrow?" Maria was starting summer by going on tour to California with her a cappella group, the Undertones.

"Naw, man, the time approacheth. So let's go to the lake. People are hanging out and I'm sure like five hipsters are playing guitar." She took off and Pete and I followed.

Our last final had ended only a few minutes before, and we were already on our way to the lakeshore. A perfect summer was already underway.

– – –

The waves of Lake Michigan lapped gently at the rocky shore, sparkling in the sun. The day was warm and breezy, as spring moved into summer.

"My tour is gonna be so crazy!" Maria yelled. "Ugh!" She had repeated this exact same thought again and again on our way to the lake, and a few more times after we sat down.

"We heard you the fifth time," I said, winking.

"Well, don't do anything I wouldn't do," Pete said.

"Actually, I think I'll do *the opposite* of what you'd do, Grandpa!" Maria smirked. This was their relationship. They were constantly teasing each other, like siblings who have spent too much time under one roof. I'd always wondered if there was another layer to that teasing, if there were some pheromones in the air. But I tried not to dwell on that.

"What are you doing this summer anyway, Pete? You didn't really say," asked Maria.

"Eh, I dunno," Pete shrugged. His smile faded a little. We waited for him to say more. Instead, we just listened to the lake breeze brush through the grass, and gently rattle the tree branches above us, just beginning to bear buds. "I think I might do a few weeks at the camp I worked at in high school. But other than that . . ."

"Well, even just sleeping for three months sounds pretty thrilling to me," I offered.

"Totally," Pete said, a smile returning to his face, though it looked a little forced. I knew he was from the wealthier North Shore suburbs of Chicago, but otherwise Pete hadn't said much about his hometown or his home life. I was never sure if he just found it boring, or if there was something really unpleasant about it.

"You know, it's so weird, I'm only about forty miles from home, but I feel like it's a world away," I said. Barrington, Illinois, my hometown, was where I felt far more comfortable than anywhere else. Northwestern was pretty good, but it wasn't home. Not yet. "I can't wait to see Cooper and Ian!" I said, beaming. I imagined how it would feel, opening the door to my house tomorrow, and having those two golden doodles bound into my arms. They still behaved like the little puppies they once were, though by now they each weighed almost eighty pounds.

"And your mom," Pete said. I looked at him, and met his glance. It always amazed me, how much he remembered about me, how much he listened when I talked. He was right. I was excited to see my mom—and I knew how excited my mom was to see me. She was still adjusting to being totally alone—a single mom *and* an empty nester. She'd gotten used to being a single mom by now—it had been twelve years, after all—but with me, her only child, out of the house, all she had was Cooper and Ian. And that wasn't quite enough for her. In fact, I realized, *she* might beat those two dogs to the door and leap into my arms first.

"When do you start working with Professor Grady?" Pete asked me. My summer wasn't going to be as chill as Pete's. I would be working with my favorite English professor, Catherine Grady, on a piece she was writing for *The Atlantic* about safe spaces and free speech on campus. She was a great writer, but she needed a research assistant. Luckily I'd made a good enough impression on her over the year that she trusted me now.

"Like, next Monday," I said. "Ten days." I grimaced a little. The thought of my summer being so compressed wasn't great.

"Ouch," Maria said, wincing.

"It'll be worth it, though," Pete said warmly. "She really likes you, and she's a big deal."

I nodded, thankful for Pete's encouragement. The three of us fell silent again—until a Frisbee sailed over towards us and perfectly smacked Pete in the face.

"Agh!" Pete yelled.

"My bad, guys!" came a full-throated baritone voice I knew all too well. It was Anthony Troy, a junior English major who rode around campus on a skateboard carrying well-worn copies of Dostoyevsky and Thomas Hardy. One of *those* guys. I'd never had a boyfriend before, and I didn't know Anthony well enough to see him that way . . . but I *did* feel like I understood thousands of cheesy songs on the radio whenever he was around.

"No prob, Bob," Maria said. She grabbed the Frisbee and tossed it back to him as he walked toward us.

"Thanks," Anthony said. "You okay, bud?"

Pete blushed. "Oh, definitely! That was funny," he sputtered.

"For sure, for sure," Anthony said in his easygoing SoCal twang. "Hey—I know you, right?"

I looked up. Anthony was looking at me. And he was expecting some kind of response. *I* certainly knew *him*, but . . .

"Yeah, uh, Morson's Russian Lit, fall quarter. We were in the same discussion section."

"Oh God, yeah," Anthony said, smiling. "That TA was such a jerk."

I laughed—*way* too loud. "Right?!"

He nodded. "Um, for sure—hey, we're just tossing over here, you guys wanna join?"

Some guy in a frat tank bellowed from the Frisbee crowd. "Troy, what's happening over there? We gonna keep playing, or—"

"Yeah, yeah," Anthony yelled back. "Come on, guys."

We looked at each other, all silently assented, and went with him.

I'm probably the least athletic person ever, but after eighteen years of being the least athletic person ever, you get good at laughing about it. Every single time somebody threw me the Frisbee, I dropped it. Every time I threw it, it went about six feet before angling sideways and kamikaze-ing straight into the ground.

"Came in fourth in the Olympic trials!" I yelled, smiling. "Twenty-twenty's my year!" Everybody laughed. Anthony bent down and picked up the Frisbee (I wasn't even *trying* to throw it to him, but of course that's where it went).

"For sure," Anthony said. That was when I looked over at Pete next to me. Suddenly his Wildcats sweatshirt, which usually fit well around his wiry frame, looked big on him. He looked like a little boy wearing his dad's old clothes. He wasn't smiling much, either.

"Hey," I whispered, "you okay?"

He looked back at me. "*Fur shur*" Pete muttered, in a dead-on impression of Anthony Troy. He smirked.

Is he jealous? I wondered. *He can't be . . . why would he be?* I looked back to the group of Anthony Troy's friends, still passing the Frisbee around. Suddenly I felt weird about being there.

"I'm gonna go, I think," I muttered, feeling flustered.

"I'll come with you," Maria said. Pete followed right behind her.

We quietly walked back to our spot on the grass, and started packing up our stuff. I could just sense Pete's tension.

"What time is it?" Maria asked. "I should probably jet." I took out my phone to check—only to find six missed calls, all from the same number. A number I didn't have in my phone. A number that was apparently from Dallas, Texas.

"What the—?" I started.

"What?" asked Pete, coming over to me. I showed him the phone. "Whoa," he said, his mouth agape. "You know anybody in Texas?"

"Texas?" Maria asked. "Wait, what's up?"

"I have all these missed calls, all from the last like ten minutes," I said. "But there's no . . . "

"There's no what?" Pete asked.

"I thought there wasn't, but . . . it just showed up. There's a voicemail. That number just left me a voicemail." This was confusing. *Telemarketers don't usually leave voicemails.*

"Snap, it's two-thirty," Maria said. "Gotta go. Bye, loves!" She hugged Pete and me quickly.

"Bye, Maria. Have a great time," Pete said. "Don't do—"

"Anything you *would* do, yep, got it," Maria said, smiling. "Good luck with your stalker or whatever."

"Ha, thanks," I managed. "Text us sometime, okay, we want to know you're alive."

Maria nodded, flashed her trademark peace sign, and was gone. Pete and I were quiet. I just kept looking at my phone. The little red "1" floating above the voicemail had put me surprisingly on edge.

"You gonna listen to that?" Pete asked.

"I guess. Stay here with me?" I said. I knew Pete would. Pete always stays.

"Whatever you need," he said. I pressed play on the voicemail and put the phone up to my ear.

"Hi there, Sara," a man's voice began. I thought I recognized it, but . . . no way, *that* would be crazy.

"Hope you're doing all right—you know, your voice-mail message was the first time I've heard your voice in twelve years. And I guess it's been that long since you've heard mine. Anyway—"

I dropped the phone. My hands were weak. My blood ran cold. Pete grabbed my shoulders. "Whoa, whoa, what's up?" he stammered. I couldn't respond. My jaw felt frozen shut. I just stared ahead. "Sara?" Pete was panicked. "Sara?"

I heard myself start to speak, as if I were very far away. "That was . . . that was my dad."

Chapter Two

"Your *WHAT?*" Pete exclaimed, his mouth agape. "But you haven't heard from him in—"

"I *know*," I snapped. And I did know, I knew exactly how long it had been since I had last spoken to him—twelve years, almost to the day. The day he walked out of my house, carrying everything he owned in two big suitcases. Hot tears streamed down my face as I watched him climb into his truck and pull away. It was a sunny summer morning—a day that everybody else in the neighborhood was thrilled about. Our street echoed with the giggles of kids chasing each other through well-mown lawns, and the raised voices of moms calling after them.

The memory of that morning came rushing back to me as Pete stared into my eyes. I couldn't help it. The pain, the confusion, the feeling that my childhood had been cut short in one instant—

My phone rang again, buzzing frantically in my hand. It was that number again: Dallas, Texas. I looked back at Pete, wild-eyed. He met my gaze, and his green eyes were amazingly calm. With Pete's strength at my back, I pressed the green button and held the phone up to my ear.

"Hey," I whispered.

"Sara! Oh, thank goodness," my dad blubbered. "How are you?"

I wasn't sure how to answer that. I was a lot of things, but I had no words to describe them.

"Of course, I know this is a lot to take in," he said. "I know." I nodded my head in silence, forgetting he couldn't see me. He sounded different. Twelve years in Dallas had given him a twang I didn't like.

"Yeah," I managed to say.

"So," he said after a pause, "you're probably wondering why I called. I'll keep it brief, I promise, but—"

"What is wrong with you? It's been twelve years!" I blurted out. It was out of my mouth before I even thought it. He went silent on the other end of the line. Pete's jaw fell open. A couple girls a few feet away looked over at me.

"I know," he finally said. "I know."

"Why didn't you ever call?"

"You think I didn't want to?" he asked. I could already hear my dad's fire coming out in his voice. He's always been quick to anger.

"So why didn't you?" I shot back.

"Well, honey," he said, "let's just say your mother didn't make it easy."

I wasn't going to back down. "Okay, that's fine, but I'm an adult now. She doesn't make all my decisions for me anymore."

"Well, your mom presented one major obstacle

along the way. She wouldn't give me your phone number. So that made it hard to reach out."

"Well, you got my number somehow, I see."

He sighed. "She relented. Because this . . . this isn't just any old phone call. This is pretty important, and she came around to see my side of things."

A shiver ran up my spine. Did I actually want to know why he was calling? A voice in my head told me to hang up right then and there and block his number. But, nonetheless, I couldn't stop myself from asking, "So, what's so important, then?"

A heavy silence hung between us. Right when I was about to ask if he was still there, he stammered, "Um, well, honey . . . I'm getting married."

I almost dropped my phone again. Two big surprises in as many minutes were making my head spin. Pete saw my reaction in my eyes. He lurched forward to catch me if I fell.

"Whoa," I said.

"I know, it's a shock," Dad said. "But I want you to

know—and this is why I called—I really want you to be there, Sara. Both Teresa and I—"

"Teresa?"

"Teresa, my fiancée. She and I really want you to be there, honey. And like you just said, you're all grown up now. You can make your own choices. You can come down here on your own without your mother."

"You already called Mom. What did she say?"

"You can imagine how that went," he said darkly.

I could, he was right. It was probably a thirty-second conversation filled with four-letter words you can't say on TV.

"Well . . . " I started. "This is a lot."

"Of course it is. I wanted to tell you, so you have at least a little time to make this decision, and be down here in time—which, again, Teresa and I would love nothing more."

"When is it?" I asked. Something told me that—

"Yeah, that's the thing. It's on Sunday," he said. I laughed, loudly. It was all I could do. *Of course it is!*

"It's Wednesday!" I yelled.

"Look, it's no big thing, we're not planning a huge bash or anything. Just a small family affair in a park by our house. But it's exactly what we want."

I felt like I had been thrown onto a carousel spinning at a thousand miles an hour. "Dad, I have to go," I said.

"Oh," he said. He sounded hurt.

"But I'll think about it," I offered. I wasn't sure I actually would, or that I even *could* without feeling sick.

"Well, I guess that's all I can ask for."

" . . . Okay then," I said. "Bye." I hung up, put my phone in my pocket, and shuddered. *What just happened?*

Pete stood stock-still, his face frozen in an expression of total confusion. And as always, he said exactly what was in my head. "What just happened?"

"I know, right?" I said. Somehow, I smiled. I looked at Pete, for the first time in what felt like an eternity. *Thank God he's here,* I thought. He smiled back, and

I laughed. "This is too crazy!" I shouted. "You can't *write* this stuff!"

– – –

"Well, it's pretty obvious," I said, my mouth half full of a delicious, greasy hamburger. Pete and I sat across from each other at Edzo's, the best burger joint in Evanston. I clutched the giant sandwich in my hand, piled high with veggies and onion strings. I hadn't realized how hungry I was until that first bite.

"It's not obvious to me," Pete said. He never talked with his mouth full, not ever. "Are you gonna go, or not?"

I swallowed forcefully. I felt my muscles tighten all over my body. "Of course not," I said. I couldn't help but sound angry. I was. *Really? You know how I feel about my dad.*

"I know, you guys have a bad history," Pete said.

"Dude, you don't know the half of it," I cut in. I took a huge bite of my burger and stared back at him, trying to will him to stop talking. This would *not* turn into a bigger discussion. "Outside of the alimony payments he has to make once a month and an Amazon gift card for my birthday every year, he hasn't been a part of my life for twelve whole years. I really only have to think about him once a year, and even once is way too much. You think I want to *see* that person? You think I want to make that person happy?"

"You're just deciding so quickly," Pete pressed on. "I know it's hard, but—"

"Dude!" I yelled, but instead of really saying a word, I just sprayed food across the table. Bits of half-chewed burger, avocado, and tomato rained down on the greasy tabletop.

Pete guffawed, holding his hand up to avoid any shrapnel. "Nice!"

My face turned hot, and I frantically grabbed napkins to clean up the mess. Pete and I were close but I still got embarrassed around him sometimes. After I had calmed down a bit, I tried again. "Why are you driving so hard at this? He's a jerk, Pete. He totally ditched me and my mom and never looked back."

"I know," Pete said quietly.

"It's like impressive or whatever that he wants to try again with me," I said. "It's big of him. But that doesn't mean I have to do the same thing."

"Yep," Pete said. "Totally." We were quiet for a while, chewing at our food, our eyes searching the walls covered in kitschy Northwestern posters and crafts. I could always tell when Pete was thinking something. He bit at his lower lip ever so slightly, but I had seen him do it often enough by now that I could spot it in an instant.

"Okay, what?" I said.

"What?" he said, taken aback. "Nothing!"

"I see you gnawing at your lip, man. Out with it, before you chew it off."

He smiled guiltily. "You know me too well." He put down his food and looked straight into my eyes, unblinking. His emerald-green eyes caught the light coming in through the big windows, and just like earlier on the lake shore, that simple gaze made me feel like I was standing on rock-solid ground.

"You're an adventurous person, Sara. In everything you do. You take really hard classes and push yourself to take on ideas and viewpoints that aren't your own. You go to parties where you don't know anybody and you come out with ten new friends. And I get that this is a whole other thing, this is like . . . *earth-shattering*. But this is the kind of thing where you excel, where you're better than most people. So just . . . " He paused, gnawed at his lip again. "Okay, that's it. Speech done."

My eyes turned hot, my vision turned blurry. *Oh, God,* I thought, *don't cry here, not in this greasy burger joint—get it together!*

"But what if it's terrible? What if he just turns his back on me all over again? I don't want to get my hopes up, because that could really easily happen, you know."

Pete nodded. "You're right, you're totally right." He said nothing more, giving me time and space to think. He took delicate bites of his burger and patiently watched me think.

"But what do I have to lose?" I asked. "At the very least I'll just be able to make the decision for myself to never talk to him again, instead of letting my mom make that decision for me."

Pete smiled. "You're Sara Jackson," he said. "You're untouchable."

I waved him off and smiled, despite myself. "Oh my God, whatever." I drummed my fingers on the table-top, ready to move on to another, more fun discussion topic. "Dessert?"

– – –

As I made the familiar turns through my neighborhood, getting closer to my house—left on Sheridan, right on Wabonsia, second exit on the traffic circle—I planned out the conversation in my head.

I'd start simple and strong. *Mom,* I'd say, *I really want to go.*

No, that wouldn't work. She'd counter right away with *Honey, I know you do, but trust me, I know your father. This won't go as planned.*

Okay, maybe I'd start another way. *Mom, Dad and I really talked for a long time about it. I actually think he'd be really heartbroken if I weren't there.*

No, that still wouldn't work. She'd say, *Well, for God's sake, don't do it for him, you and I don't owe him jack!*

I made a right at the light on Route 9, cruised past the Panera and the empty storefront where the ice cream place used to be. I was getting close to home, and I still didn't know how I could convince my mom I should go.

I wasn't sure I had even convinced myself. Did I only care about pleasing my dad? I certainly didn't owe him anything—but I really didn't even *know* him. I was a completely different person now than I was when he left. Maybe this version of me could handle this trip. Could it be fun? Or would it just be painful? Would I feel included? Or completely lonely?

Yet, despite all that, something pulled me towards saying yes. No matter how much I tried to convince myself it would be too sad, too unsettling . . .

And there it was, my childhood home, one seventy-nine Glenwood Avenue. And looking at the little white house, I realized it was the same as my dad would remember it, from twelve years before. Not even a fresh coat of paint to cover up the chipped wood siding since he left.

I parked the car in the driveway, launched myself out of the driver's seat, and bounded towards the door. *No time like the present,* I said, trying to strengthen myself.

But as soon as I opened the door, I was ruined. My strength left me. There was my mom, sitting on the couch, a box of Kleenex in front of her, stray tissues balled up around her like little lonely clouds.

"Whoa, Mom, is everything—"

"Oh, honey!" my mom exclaimed, brushing off her cheeks. "I wasn't expecting you!"

Before she could answer, Cooper and Ian bounded

out of the back part of the house, charging towards me with all their might. They both jumped up on their hind legs to unleash a barrage of kisses.

"Hi, hi!" I squealed, giggling. No matter how far away you went or how long you were gone, these boys would never hold a grudge. I wrapped my arms around them and rubbed their soft curly blond fur. Now *this* was home.

But I knew I couldn't relax while my mom remained on the couch, looking distraught. I let the dogs down and sat down on the couch next to her.

"What's happening? Why are you crying?" She looked up at me, her blue eyes wet with tears. She threw her arms around me and moaned. Her body felt small and bony and her arms and back were trembling.

"Mom, what is it?"

"He . . . Did he call you?"

"Yeah," I said. "He told me about the wedding, he wants me to come. All the same stuff he told you, I guess. But I'm okay, don't worry—"

"Oh, I'm just so angry at him!" my mom bellowed.

Her hands flew up to her face, pulled at her powder-gray hair.

"For getting remarried? I'm sure that really stings—"

"For manipulating you like that! He's just doing it to twist the knife with me. I'm sure of it! But I let him sweet-talk me into giving him your phone number. This sob story about how he's lost touch with you and this is such a big moment for him . . . ahh!" She sobbed, doubling over and holding her face in her hands.

I sighed. *This is gonna be much, much harder than I thought.*

"Mom, relax," I said firmly. She looked up at me like I had just insulted her. "If he *is* doing it to make you unhappy, I'm sorry, and that's wrong of him. But I do think he really does want me to go." I swallowed hard. Here it was. "And . . . I want to go. To the wedding."

My mother stared at me like she had just seen a ghost. Like I was some alien clone of myself. A thick silence hung in the air between us. Her upper lip trembled. Her eyes frantically searched the eggshell-colored walls.

"Ah," she stammered, barely audible.

"I know," I said.

She snapped back to look at me, her eyes hard. "No, I don't think you do," she spat. "You can't know—you haven't even *seen* him in twelve years! I'm sure you barely recognized his voice today!" I had to admit, she was right about that.

"But that's why I want to go," I said. "Don't you think I should get to know him? He *is* my father, like it or not."

"Honey," my mom started, obviously trying to calm down. She grasped my hand in hers, which were cold and clammy and still trembling with emotion. "I know you think that is what you want, but trust me. It's fine if you want to get to know him. I won't get in the way of that. But this isn't the way to do it."

"Why?" Though I was feeling sorry for my mom

and how sad all this had made her, I was starting to lose patience with getting shut down again and again.

"It just isn't! Honey, I've been on this earth a little longer than you have."

"That isn't a reason! I'm an adult now, I can make my own choices, and I *choose* to go, to meet his wife and her family—and, honestly, meet *him* for the first time." I didn't lose eye contact with my mom. I stayed strong. "Almost everyone I've ever known has a dad. Or two parents, at least. And it's not that you weren't enough, Mom, it's not about that. But I've always wondered what having someone else would be like . . . and now I get to find out. Does that make sense?"

Slowly, Mom matched my gaze, but looked distant. Maybe she was finally coming around.

But instead, after a moment, she said, "Do you want some dinner? There's a whole plateful of spaghetti carbonara I couldn't eat, I was *so* full." Before I could answer, she got up and walked into the kitchen. I flopped back on the couch, letting her have some space.

As she clattered around in the kitchen, I found my thoughts drifting back to a softball game in sixth grade. It was one of the few games my mom couldn't come to. For the first time, I had nobody in the stands. And when the game ended, and everybody's parents came and patted them on the back, all I could do was watch. I had walked the mile home that night—slowly, trying to picture where my dad was and what he was doing instead of emptying the Gatorade cooler with the team or playing catch with me as we walked to the car under an orange sky, the air filled with the buzz of cicadas.

But it's hard to picture someone you barely know.

— — —

I walked into the kitchen to find Mom gingerly stirring a pot of pasta. "Mom," I said softly. "Heat's not on." She blushed and looked under the pot.

"Oh," she said. "You're right." She turned the knob and the heating coil slowly turned red. We were silent again for a minute, until she murmured, "I guess I always hoped I was enough for you."

A lump bubbled in my throat and my eyes watered. I grabbed her hand. "Mom, of *course* you were! You *are!* I'm not doing this because you've been, like, inadequate or something."

She looked up at me, tears in her eyes. She was fumbling for words.

"I really think it could be good, Mom," I said. I wasn't going to let this go.

"Honey," she started, taking a deep breath, "I know you do. And I love you for that, I love your optimism. But, so sue me, I don't want to see you get hurt."

"I won't."

"You might."

I felt my blood start to boil. She *still* wasn't listening to me! I forced myself to take a deep breath. "You let me go off to college this year. And I've done pretty okay there, right?"

Mom didn't answer. She just kept stirring the pasta in slow circles. "Right?" I offered again.

She shook her head gently, a small smile creeping across her face. "You amaze me."

"I know," I said. I hugged her, squeezing her bony shoulders tight. "Wow, I am *so* much taller than you. When did that happen? Either I'm still growing or you've started shrinking!"

"Oh, stop," she said, batting me away.

While I ate my mom's leftover pasta—alongside a glass of chocolate milk, nothing stronger allowed in Mom's household—we kept talking. After she had at least tentatively given her support to the Texas trip, we managed to talk about other, more fun things. About school, about my friends, about the A I got on a paper defending *Harry Potter* as a work of third-wave feminist fiction. The warmth of home finally crept in, as the hours ticked by: nine, ten, eleven, twelve . . .

My mom started yawning at twelve-thirty, so I decided bedtime was in order. But I realized there was one thing we hadn't discussed.

"How long would it take to drive there?" I asked. "Plane tickets will be too expensive, so . . . "

"Whoa, honey, that's a long way—"

"Two days? Maybe three?"

"But I don't want you doing that on your own. That's not safe. You're a pretty young woman and you've never done a road trip on your own—"

I already knew what I would do. "I won't be alone. I'll take someone with me." It was so obvious. He would say yes, no doubt.

Chapter Three

"RISE AND SHINE!" I CROWED OUT OF MY driver's-side window. Pete stood in the driveway clutching an overstuffed duffel bag, squinting in the early morning sun. After we'd spent Thursday at home packing, Friday was here—the day we had to put up or shut up, and hit the road.

"Hey," he said happily. "You bring doughnuts?"

"Yep, straight out of the ovens at Bennison's," I shot back giddily. It was barely seven, sure—and I'd had to drive an hour to Pete's house in Lake Forest— but I had all the energy of a kid on Christmas morning.

Pete approached the car and slung his bag in the

backseat. "That thing's packed to the gills," I said. "What'd you bring, dude?"

"I always overpack," Pete said modestly.

"This old thing gonna make it to Texas and back?" came a booming voice. It was Pete's dad, Paul. (Pete's mom was named Mary, and she and Paul were big fans of a certain folk group from the 1960s. Naming their only son Peter was the obvious choice).

"Hey, Mr. Carlson," I said, beaming. Pete's dad was like Santa Claus on happy pills every day of the year. And just like his son, he wore Northwestern swag every day. Today was a big purple T-shirt pronouncing him a "Proud Northwestern Grandma," something I figured he got on sale at the bookstore. Paul had a completely zany sense of humor that hadn't quite been passed on to his son.

"What is this, a ninety-nine?" he asked me.

"Dad, chill," Pete said, rubbing his temples.

"A two-thousand one, actually," I said. "Not quite so old."

"Ah yes, two-thousand one, a great year for Toyota

Corollas," Paul said, laughing. "Well, I won't ask you how many miles you got on there," he said, "but if the odometer has too many zeroes to count, I recommend you take a bus." He patted the roof of the car, waiting for us to laugh. I offered a smile. Pete didn't even take his eyes off the floor of the car, like he was trying to shut his dad up via Jedi mind trick.

"All right, well, check in with us every so often, okay?" Paul asked, now a little more serious. "It's a long drive—and Texans are a whole 'nother species!" he crowed.

"Thanks for letting Pete come with me," I said. "This whole thing is pretty crazy. Good thing he's such an awesome friend." I looked over at Pete as I said this. He blushed, like he always did.

"Hey, our pleasure. We get pretty sick of him after a couple days!"

"Thanks, Pops," Pete said.

"Well, you better get going, eh? Get some barbecue for me," Paul said. "I love you, Peter, be safe."

"Yep," Pete said.

"He loves you, too," I said, winking. I put the car in gear, and pulled out of the driveway.

"You okay?" I asked.

"What? Oh, yeah. No, I'm fine." Pete ran a hand through his copper-red hair and looked out the window. "Just tired!" He grabbed my phone from the cup-holder. "Want me to pull up some directions?" he asked.

My stomach lurched. "Um, actually, could you use your phone? Mine's already low on battery," I said.

I was lying. I didn't want Pete looking at my phone for a very specific reason. I woke up to a few texts earlier that morning from Maria, asking about the situation with my dad. I told her everything, that he was getting married, that I was going to go, and that Pete was going to come with me.

Wait . . . really? she asked.

Uh . . . yeah? What? I typed back.

Just you and Pete? idk that might be a little awk right?

Why?

Ugh honestly sara. He has such a thing for you.

…?!

Come on, you know it.

But we're just friends wtf

Sara you can be friends and something ELSE too ya know

You're just assuming things. We're close and everything ya but that's not what's up, trust me. You're reading into things

With that, our talk was over. And even though it was hours ago now, I was still a little edgy about it. It had really rubbed me the wrong way. Who was she to tell me about my friendship with Pete? He and I were closer than I'd ever been with any other friend. If people fell in love with best friends, those songs on the radio about how confusing love was wouldn't exist. It was that simple.

I forced the issue out of my mind. Here we were, finally hitting the road. There were doughnuts, there was a full tank of gas, and a long way to drive. And

Pete was next to me. He was my best friend. Nothing more.

"Sure, no problem," Pete said, taking out his phone. "Destination: Dallas."

– – –

A warm June day bloomed all around us as we sped south through Illinois. Outside of Chicago, the land flattened and spread straight out to the horizon line. Without the tall buildings in the way, we could see to what looked like the ends of the earth, with only the occasional silo or suburban strip mall to block the view. The sun, free of clouds, shone down on the car, and into my eyes behind the wheel.

For the first three hours of our trip, Pete snoozed openmouthed against the window. *So much for keeping me entertained,* I mused.

But I didn't hate having the time to reflect. *I've never really left home,* I realized. Sure, I'd traveled on trips with my mom, and with my high school choir, but that was kid stuff. And even Northwestern was practically in my backyard. My hour-long drive home was nothing compared to my friend Jae, who flew home to South Korea on holiday breaks. This was a whole new thing.

Pete roused me from my meditation. "Whoa, what's happening?" he stammered, still half asleep.

"Wakey-wakey," I said, smiling. "Welcome to southern Illinois."

"We're in the middle of nowhere," he said, blinking in the sunlight.

"Exactly. Pretty cool, right?"

He looked out at the landscape. "We got any more doughnuts?"

I shook my head. "You only have yourself to blame for that one, dude."

I was waiting for Pete to say something sassy back, but instead he sat straight up and looked out his window, like a dog after a mail truck. "Wow, I woke up just in time!" he shouted.

"What are you talking about?" I asked, on edge.

"Look!" He pointed to a shape in the distance. I squinted, unsure of what I was looking at . . . but then it dawned on me. We were closing in on the border of Missouri, which meant we were closing in on St. Louis, which meant we were closing in on the giant Gateway Arch! *That* was what we were looking at! It towered in the distance, a portal to the smack-dab middle of the country.

"Whoa," I whispered. It was even more majestic than in all the photos I'd seen. It looked like a huge chrome horseshoe, thrown down from space and stuck straight in the earth.

"Want to take a break and go get some pictures?" Pete asked. The last time I'd seen him this happy was when the Northwestern football team *almost* beat Michigan State. ("Still, such an achievement!")

His enthusiasm worked on me. "I could use a break anyway," I said.

After fighting traffic in the city and searching desperately for parking, Pete and I finally found ourselves in front of the Gateway Arch—or, really, underneath it. We both stared upwards, craning our necks to get the full effect.

"It looks like it just sort of disappears, doesn't it?" Pete said, his eyes searching the sky. He was right. It was so tall that from where we stood, it looked like it never ended.

I looked over at him. "Thanks for being here with me," I said. Pete and I usually made jokes and teased each other, but that moment—standing in a place I'd never been, looking at a monument the whole world can recognize—softened me. It felt weird, being so . . . sentimental.

"Stop saying that!" Pete laughed. "It's not like I'm here just putting in community service hours or something."

I took out my phone and opened up Instagram. "Pics or it didn't happen, right?" I joked. I held out the phone and Pete bent down close to me for a selfie. He put his arm around my waist as he ducked for the photo—his hand was warm from the sun, and I felt it through my thin cotton T-shirt. I shuddered as goosebumps raised on my skin, frigid from the car's AC. I leaned into his hand, just a little bit.

I snapped the photo. "We have to nail the hashtag," Pete said. He was right.

"We'll workshop it in the car," I said. We had a long way to go.

– – –

By seven o'clock that night, we were about fifty miles from Springfield, Missouri, not far from the Oklahoma border. Both Pete and I were weary after a full day on the road. Empty McDonald's bags were scattered around the front seat. Pete had taken over driving a few hours before, and from the way his skinny fingers gripped the steering wheel, he looked like he was fighting the urge to sleep.

"I hate to be that guy," Pete said, "but how much farther are we going today?"

"We should stop in Springfield," I said. "I wanted to get to Oklahoma, but that's okay."

"Haha, 'OK,'" Pete said, "get it?" I looked at him blankly. "Like, the initials of the state? . . . Yeah, I know, not my best."

"The master of the Dad Joke, Pete Carlson," I said. He bowed his head.

"Do you want me to take over driving?" I asked. He looked at me like a pathetic puppy dog. "*Okay*," I said, winking.

As I drove, I couldn't help but feel a little distracted. My mind wandered back to Maria's texts earlier in the day. *Sara you can be friends and something ELSE ya know.* My stomach tightened up in a tiny knot. That's not what was going on between us. Right? The fun, easy banter Pete and I had in the car was the same we always had. The kinds of jokes best friends share. I was determined to keep my guard up. If anything changed between us—a weird look, a hug that went on too long—I'd call him on it. I was sure of it.

Eventually SPRINGFIELD: NEXT EXIT appeared on a road sign, and I prepared to turn off the highway. "Hey, Mr. Sulu, want to find us a place to crash?"

Pete had been zoning out, staring out the window, and my words startled him. "Sorry," he said, "I was getting pretty close to finding Jesus out there." He chuckled, and pulled out his phone. Seconds later, he had a place picked out—the Welcome Inn, whose website promised *Affordable Rates and Flexible Dates, In One of America's Greatest States!*

"I appreciate their modesty," Pete said. "'One of the greatest states.' It's hard to argue with that. I'd say Missouri might be in the top . . . twenty-five?"

We pulled into the parking lot, which was populated by just a few cars. The motel was not large. It was just one story with maybe twelve rooms, which at the moment were all dark. "Puttin' on the Ritz," Pete said under his breath.

Inside the shabby, fluorescent-lit lobby, we were greeted by a middle-aged woman wearing a worn-out T-shirt featuring a wolf howling at a big yellow moon. She seemed positively thrilled to see us. "Why, hi there!" she boomed.

"Hey," Pete and I said simultaneously.

"Y'all been drivin'?" she asked, eager to start a conversation. I could only imagine how many hours she'd been sitting in here alone.

"Yep, all day. We started today in Chicago," I said.

"Well I'll be gol-danged—sorry, pardon my French—but my, that's quite a long way! Y'all deserve a beauty rest then."

"You're preaching to the choir," Pete said, trying his hand at a down-home saying. The woman looked back at him somewhat blankly, and then asked a question I was not at all prepared to answer.

"Single room, then?"

I looked over at Pete, Maria's texts rising in the back of my mind. I squelched them. Best friends could share a bedroom, no problem. This would be a breeze. "If you're cool, I'm cool," I said.

Pete shrugged, not a note of tension or awkwardness in his face. "Totes."

– – –

Half an hour later, when Pete and I laid down next to each other in the king bed, I realized the only time I'd ever shared a bed with *anyone* had been with my mom, on our road trip to California a few years ago.

But even though I was *technically* getting into bed with a boy, the situation didn't feel entirely too different. I wished I could text Maria and fully describe how wrong she was about this situation, but I thought better of risking Pete looking at my phone. We got as comfortable as possible on the cheap, scratchy sheets. We settled into our far sides of the mattress, leaving a wide gulf between us.

After scrolling through my phone for a while, perusing the various photos of Maria and her a cappella group in California, I muttered, "My literal entire newsfeed is pictures of the Undertones."

Pete snickered on the other side of the bed. He put on an annoying hyper-girly voice and said, "Hashtag tones-tour!"

Eventually my eyelids drooped and I turned off the light on my side of the bed. "Good night," I said, smiling at Pete and pulling the covers up around my chin. "I'm glad you're here."

He flashed his little gap-toothed smile. "Me too," he said, switching off his light.

"Night," I said. I closed my eyes, and even though I felt dead tired, sleep did not come easily. Sights and sounds of my dad, and of my parents together, exploded around my mind. Each one flashed by too quickly for me to grab onto.

Finally, one image of my dad settled and I lived inside of it. There he was, looking down at me, smiling, against a clear blue sky. His salt-and-pepper hair parted from left to right, his scruffy tan face spreading outward in his big goofy grin. "Good try, Sara," he said in his deep baritone. "You left it all on the field. That's the mark of a great athlete." He tousled my hair, his big tough hands warm on my head.

Where did *that* dad go? How did *that* dad become the dad who turned his back on us, carrying those two suitcases out to his truck, never to return? Maybe he was that dad all along—selfish, angry, bitter—but he hid it. He hid it so well that I actually managed to trust him. To love him. How different my life would be if he had had the decency to leave when I was an infant, or before I was even born. Instead I had to live with that image of him walking away, that image that made my head ache, made my eyes hot and dewy.

Suddenly Pete let out a forceful burst of a snore. *He was already asleep? How?!* But he rolled over and quieted down. He looked peaceful.

I didn't remember falling asleep that night, but I guess I did, because when my alarm went off at seven-thirty, I sat straight up. It took a few panicked seconds to remember where in the world I was. My Wildcats T-shirt clung to me, damp with sweat. At some point during the night the cheap AC unit in the room had turned off. Then I realized I was sitting in the middle of the bed. I had edged toward Pete during the night. We weren't more than six inches apart now, as he slumbered on, deaf to the alarm. He hadn't noticed how close we'd gotten, and neither had I.

Chapter Four

THE DAY WAS OVERCAST AND MUGGY, PRESENTING nothing like the inviting landscape that had greeted us the day before. Pete started out behind the wheel, and for the first hour of the day we sat quietly, eating our unhealthy breakfast of sludgy coffee and plastic bowls full of dry Frosted Flakes from a gas station outside Joplin.

We approached the Oklahoma border around ten, and as we got closer Pete perked up in the driver's seat. "I love seeing places for the first time," he said earnestly. "Don't you?" A big blue sign came into view on our right-hand side. *Oklahoma! Discover the Excellence,* it screamed.

"Oh, we will!" Pete shouted, honking the horn as we blew past the sign.

I couldn't help but chuckle. "Where is it?" I giggled. "I'm trying to discover it!"

"I don't know, that busted-up farmhouse over there is *pretty* excellent," Pete said dryly.

"Something tells me there's more where that came from," I said.

"We're being a little hard on Oklahoma," Pete said. "I'm sure it's . . . " He winked at me, letting me finish the joke.

"'OK,'" I said. We both threw our heads back and cackled, and Pete honked the horn again giddily.

I felt my phone buzz in my pocket. "Sorry," I said, flustered. I pulled it out and looked at the name on the screen. "I'm gonna have to take this," I said to Pete, "it's my mom."

"No prob," Pete said.

I swiped right and put the phone to my ear. "Hello?"

"Oh, Sara!" came my mom's whimpering voice on the other end. "You're there!"

"What do you mean I'm *there*? Of course I'm here!"

"I've called, I don't know, six or eight times! You can't blame me for worrying."

"Oh," I said, startled. "We're out in the middle of nowhere, I must have been in and out of cell service. What's up?"

"Well I didn't hear from you at all yesterday," she said admonishingly. "I felt like I deserved a little update *today* at least!"

"Yeah, sorry about that," I said. "We were having too much fun." Pete smiled at me warmly.

Mom asked me seemingly endless questions—where we were, what we'd been eating, if I had enough money, if we'd seen any sketchy activity on the way. It was one of those conversations where she asked almost constant questions—and asked them so quickly that I knew she wasn't listening to the answers.

There was one topic, of course, I *really* hoped we could avoid. And as we got closer to the half-hour mark of the conversation, I was pretty sure I'd get off scot-free. But then she asked, "So, where did you stay last night, anyway?"

My stomach lurched. I looked over at Pete frantically, forgetting he couldn't hear the question. *What?* he mouthed.

"We found a cheap motel." I ended the sentence firmly, hoping there wouldn't be any other questions. But that was foolish.

"Oh, goodness. Well, I wish you had told me, I could have counseled you out of that—or done some research online to find one near you where you wouldn't get hepatitis!"

"Oh, come on," I said, rolling my eyes. "Neither Pete nor I are showing signs of hepatitis."

Pete's eyes bulged and he nearly lost control of the wheel. "What the—" he started.

I cut him off. "The *motel* was totally acceptable." He understood what I was talking about and relaxed.

"Separate rooms, I hope?" she asked. I could just *hear* her right eyebrow raise skeptically.

"Duh," I said, a little too quickly. There was a silence before she continued.

"Well, good. Will you make it to your father's by tonight, or should I be looking for a disease-free place for you?"

"No, we'll make it," I said. "Anyway, Pete's been driving awhile, I should take over—"

"I understand," she said. "I love you, Sara. And I am proud of you."

I smiled, a pit opening in my stomach. My heart broke for her. I pictured her sitting on that couch, the dogs at her feet, not thinking about anything other than me and my dad. "I love you too, Mom. Don't worry too much about me, okay? I'll talk to you soon."

"What was *that* about?" Pete asked as I ended the call. "She thinks we got hepatitis?"

But before I could explain, my phone buzzed to life again. "Oh my God," I said, ready to chuck my phone out the window. "What now?"

It was Dad calling this time. It was that same Dallas area code that had started this whole thing off. I showed the phone to Pete.

"Good luck," he said sweetly. I knew he really meant it.

I couldn't believe my parents' timing. Obviously, after all these years apart, they were still in sync in some ways. I took a deep breath and grew tense.

"Hello?"

"Sara, hi," came my dad's voice on the other end. His tone was brittle, like he had something he really needed to say.

"Hey," I said cautiously.

"How far have you gotten? On your drive?"

"We're actually already into Oklahoma," I said, smiling. "We're making pretty good time!"

"Ah," he said darkly. "Well . . . "

"*Well* what?" I asked. Something was wrong.

"The wedding's off."

He said it quickly, just three words, in one breath, that totally knocked me sideways. I didn't—couldn't—say anything, for what felt like an eternity.

" . . . Hello?" Dad asked nervously. "You still there?"

"Yeah," I said. "Um . . . "

"You can certainly still come if you want, honey, we'd love to have you. I'd love nothing more. Honestly."

"Uh, huh . . . "

"I really thought . . . " he began, but he trickled off. Then there were just a few soft sniffles from the other end of the line. *Oh great,* I thought, *now he's crying.*

I glanced over at Pete and mouthed "wedding," and sliced an invisible dagger across my neck. His eyes opened wide and he couldn't stop himself from bellowing, "What?!"

"Who was that?" Dad asked.

"Oh, that's Pete. My friend Pete. He's the one driving with me."

"He's your boyfr—"

"No!" I shouted, blushing. "He's just . . . we're

just friends." Pete knew from my answer what my dad asked. He grinned, looking out at the open road. I wanted to die. What *else* could possibly go wrong?

"Well," I began. "I'm not sure what to say."

"I know. Me neither, honestly," Dad said softly. I surprised myself then. I actually felt sad for him, somehow. I couldn't bring myself to ask, but it seemed like he hadn't been the one to call the wedding off.

"I'm not mad," I said.

"Really?"

"Really. I just . . . Pete and I are gonna have to discuss, okay?"

"Yes, absolutely," Dad said. He sounded hopeful.

"If we decide to keep driving, though," I said, "we'll be there by tonight. Is that too soon?"

"Not at all," he said warmly. "We'd love to have you guys anytime."

"Okay then," I said. I didn't have much else to say. How was I going to wrap this up? "Sorry . . . about your wedding." *Oof.*

"Thanks," he said. "I'll talk to you soon, then."

"Okay."

I hung up, and dropped the phone into my lap. I didn't need to tell Pete anything. He had practically heard the whole conversation. The same question I'd been asking myself for days came up again. *What were we going to do?*

— — —

The waitress practically slammed the ceramic plates, piled high with pancakes, eggs, bacon, and biscuits, down onto the greasy tabletop. Pete and I had decided to reward ourselves with a long lunch at a roadside diner. I drowned the entire plate in syrup—something I've done since I can remember—and tore away at it with my knife and fork.

Between the phone call and the diner, Pete and I hadn't said much of anything to one another, still reeling from the gigantic monkey wrench tossed into our plans. Knowing Pete, he was waiting for me to speak first. He always waited to hear what I had to say.

After swallowing three or four huge mouthfuls of food, I sat back against the red vinyl bench.

"Easy there, tiger," Pete said. He had barely made a dent in his omelet—an *egg white* omelet, full of vegetables. I rolled my eyes.

"Stress eating, ever heard of it?" I said dryly.

"What could you *possibly* have to be stressed about?" Pete asked, smirking.

I rolled my eyes. "Ha ha, very funny."

I looked out the window next to our table. On the other side of the two-lane highway, the flat, toast-brown land stretched out until it connected with the robin's-egg-blue sky. Brown stalks of tall grass blew gently in the warm wind, and a few big, dark birds circled overhead, looking for food scurrying in the dust below.

Suddenly I felt very, very far from home.

I remembered how giddy Pete had been blowing past the "Welcome to Oklahoma" road sign. How good it felt to stand in front of the arch in St. Louis. To explore the country, cut loose, take chances.

"Can I say something?" Pete asked, jolting me from my long gaze across the road. *Oh God,* I thought. *Is he going to proclaim his love for me right now? In this diner? Was Maria right?*

He continued without a response from me. "I know you're doing this because you want to get to know your dad. And I think that's great."

"But?" I asked, raising an eyebrow.

"Well . . . you've met my dad," he said. "Everybody loves him. He's got a million friends. He holds court at every party he goes to, and on and on."

"I'm sure," I said. "He's hilarious."

Pete nodded curtly. "Right."

"But?" I said again.

"He's not exactly like that . . . when the party ends. When it's just him and me and my mom and my sisters again. He's quiet, and he's distant, and he can be really mean." My heart rate slowed. Where was he going with this? "He used to make fun of me in high school, because, well . . . I mean, I'm not the most athletic person ever, right? I've been scrawny and gangly my whole life. He still calls me BP, which stands for Beat Pete, because . . . "

"I'm not sure," I said awkwardly.

Pete smiled sheepishly, running both hands through his fluffy hair. "Ah, because everybody can 'Beat Pete' in gym class."

I inhaled sharply, but was at a loss for words. Eventually I managed, "I'm sorry, Pete. That's so mean."

Pete shook his head. "I'm not saying this to, like, confess how abusive my father is. And he's not doing it to be mean, it's just . . . that's what he does. And I think every family has that kind of thing. I mean, you don't have a perfect relationship with your mom."

"Definitely not," I said.

"Right," said Pete. "So, I know you feel like you really missed out on something by not having your dad around for much of your life, and in some ways you did. But I think you're expecting to have this sunshiny friendship with him . . . and I just don't want you to be disappointed, is all." He tried to take a big final gulp of coffee but he dribbled most of it down his chin, and onto his shirt. After nervously dabbing at the spill with a fistful of napkins, he took a deep breath. "Sorry, that was a lot. Okay, I'm done now. Sorry."

I reached out and put my hand on his. "Thank you," I said. "You're right. I need to manage my expectations. And sorry your dad is such a jerk sometimes."

He shrugged, smiling. He picked up his fork again and took another bite of his omelet.

We ate in silence for a minute as I thought everything over. "You know," I said eventually, "even though the wedding isn't happening, and even if meeting my dad is super painful or awkward or whatever and we leave after forty-five minutes . . . I still want to keep driving. I want to finish what we started."

Pete smiled. "Awesome," he said. "I'm so happy to hear that."

"More coffee?" Our smoky-voiced waitress in her pale-pink uniform had appeared out of nowhere. She held the gigantic steel pot over the table.

"Sure," Pete said, pushing his mug forward.

As she poured, the waitress looked right at me. "Couldn't help but overhear," she said. "Don't shy away from pain, sweetie. Sounds crazy, I know, but trust me. Best things that ever happened to me, things that changed me the most in my life, they were real hard to go through. But you'll come through the other side better for it."

I just gawked at her, unsure of what to say.

"You'll excuse my manners," she said, giving the mug back to Pete. "Oklahomans don't mince words. Maybe you're not from around here."

"No," I managed.

"Well, I won't bother you anymore, then. Just thought I should offer my two cents."

"We appreciate it," Pete said genially. He could be so unbelievably charming.

"*There's* some Midwestern kindness," the waitress said, winking at Pete. Adults—professors, parents, you name it—always loved Pete. He always claimed he didn't know why.

"I'll leave you alone, kids," the waitress said plainly. "Just think about what I told you."

She walked away slowly, limping to one side. She looked like she had been here forever, tucked away out on the plains serving pancakes and eggs to hungry, bleary-eyed drivers. She walked to another table and poured coffee into the mugs of the family sitting there: two kids, a mom, and a dad. The classic unit.

After she was out of earshot, Pete and I looked at each other and giggled. "I think she might have been a prophet!" Pete said, laughing. Then he put on a throaty Yoda voice. "Listen to her, you should."

Chapter Five

THE HOUSE WAS BIGGER THAN I THOUGHT IT WOULD be, certainly bigger than the house I lived in with my mom. *The house where Dad used to live,* I reminded myself. His house down here in Texas was in the fancy Dallas neighborhood of Westlake. It sat on a big plot of land at the end of a cul-de-sac, and as we approached it, it just seemed to get bigger.

Two Greco-Roman columns stood tall on either side of the massive brown front door. Large bay windows peered out on the ground level beneath similarly large windows above. The house's face was made of crimson brick, smoothed down so it appeared almost fake. Maybe it was.

Only the downstairs lights were on, casting a warm glow into the darkness of the unlit neighborhood. There weren't even any other cars on the street. I pictured the neighborhood's minivans tucked away for the night, in orderly garages that smelled of spare tires and bags of sod.

I sat stock-still in the driver's seat. Pete sat next to me, neither of us talking. I just stared straight ahead, trying to wrap my mind around the fact that on the other side of that massive brown door—which looked like it had been taken from a castle in *Lord of the Rings*—sat my dad. My dad, a man who had been out of my life so long that I had actually gotten used to it.

Though my body was frozen in the driver's seat, my mind was running at a million miles an hour. Would he be wearing the same clothes he used to wear? Was he going to be fifty pounds heavier? Have a big bushy beard? Would I recognize him even if he hadn't changed at all?

"There's nothing left to do," Pete said, "but just dive in."

"I know," I said softly, not looking at him. But I didn't move a muscle. Pete shifted in his seat.

"Looks like he's doing pretty well for himself," Pete said. "This is like *Real Housewives* territory."

"Seriously," I said. "Where'd he get all this money from?"

"Let's find out, huh?" Pete reached out and took my hand. Shivers rocketed up my spine and I shuddered. But he didn't let go. "I'll be there with you."

I had a sudden impulse to grab his hand and kiss it out of sheer appreciation. *Must be the nerves making me crazy,* I thought. I shook it off, smiling at my friend. "I know, Pete. You're the best."

We clambered out of the Corolla. The car doors slammed behind us, and we walked confidently up to the front door, Pete just a few steps behind me. I found the oversized gold doorbell and pushed it. Orchestral clangs rang out throughout the house. I waited, holding my breath.

Then I heard "Aha!" from inside the house. Suddenly my mind flashed to a memory of me, five years old, standing on the front porch of our house in Illinois. I had just gotten back from my first day of kindergarten, and hopped off the bus and tottered up to our front door. I remembered how my hand wasn't big or strong enough to turn the knob, so I pressed our doorbell—our cheesy plastic doorbell. I stood there, wearing my brand-new *Power Rangers* backpack, knowing full well who was going to greet me in a moment's time—and heard "Aha!" from inside. I listened for his footsteps approaching the door. They were the steps of the leather-bottomed wool slippers he always wore inside the house, coming ever closer toward—

And then the memory clashed with the present as he flung open the front door. Only one thing was different. For the first time, I wasn't looking up at him from two feet below. Now I was looking at him head-on.

We could only manage to stare at one another. His

hazel eyes were the same as mine. Finally, I managed one word. "Hey."

"Hey," he said softly. He spread his arms out wide and I couldn't resist the invitation. I practically fell forward into him, and he wrapped his burly arms around me, clad in a thick wool sweater. I rested my head on his shoulder. *I shouldn't feel okay about this,* I thought to myself. *I should be meaner to him.* But I couldn't do it.

Finally, we separated, and I realized Pete had just been standing there watching us. "Uh," I said, frantically, "Dad, this is my friend Pete."

"Hey, Pete," Dad said, extending a hand. Pete took it and shook firmly.

"Nice to meet you, sir," Pete said.

"Oh, no, no," Dad said, "call me Danny. I insist."

"Nice to meet you . . . Danny," Pete managed.

"Come in, come in," Dad said, stepping back into the warm glow of the house. He led us through the first floor of the house, back towards the kitchen. It was like something from a magazine. High ceilings towered above the immaculate wide-open floor plan. There was a living room complete with a giant flat-screen TV on the wall and a yacht-sized three-paneled couch. Past the living room was a formal dining room with a rectangular solid-wood table. On the other side of the living room was a grand staircase with a red runner carpet up the middle, twisting upwards into the second floor, a mile away into the sky.

Dad led us into the kitchen, which was practically shimmering under the lights coming down from the ceiling. A rack of copper pots and pans hung over a gigantic granite-topped island, surrounded by leather barstools. And somehow, despite all the glamor, it was warm and inviting.

Pete and I couldn't help but walk into the room in awe, dumbstruck at the sophistication and style on display. Dad noticed our slack-jawed faces and chuckled. "Yeah, we're pretty happy with it." But his face quickly darkened, and he looked away.

But just as soon as he had darkened, he brightened again. "What can I get you? Coffee, lemonade—ooh, I have some sweet tea, now that you're in the South—or maybe you're hungry? Would you like dinner?"

"Just water for me," Pete and I said in unison. Dad raised an eyebrow at that, charmed, but said nothing.

We sat down around the island, big glasses of ice water sweating onto the granite. None of us knew where to begin.

After enough awkward silence, Dad offered, "I can't thank you enough for coming, Sara—and you, Pete, for helping out." Pete nodded softly, taking a nervous gulp of water. I'd never seen Pete look so uncomfortable, but I'm sure I looked ten times more awkward.

"I'm glad I came," I said. "Basically." *Oh God! What?!* It came out of my mouth before I had time to stop it. "I mean . . . you know . . . ," I stuttered, trying to cover my tracks.

"No problem," Dad said. "I'm glad you're glad."

Another silence set in. Pete took action. "You know what," he said, "I'm pretty tired, it's been a long day of driving. Would it be all right if I turned in for the night?"

Classic Pete, I thought. He recognized that there was a lot of talking that needed to happen without him around. I thanked him over and over again in my head, hoping he'd hear it.

"Sure thing," Dad said. "I've got you all set up in the guest room." He led Pete out of the kitchen, but on their way out, I heard him say, "Of course, you have your choice of rooms."

What did *that* mean? His choice of rooms? How many bedrooms were in this place?

A ton of questions started unspooling in my head. This was a huge house—was Dad living here with his fiancée? Where *was* she, anyway? Why did they need this much space?

My heart quickened as I realized there could only be one answer to any of these questions. I started looking around the kitchen to see if I was right. The room was so tidy that nothing was immediately obvious. But I made my way to the giant stainless steel fridge and opened the door, searching the shelves.

My dad came back into the room behind me. "Looking for something to eat?" He asked.

I turned around to face him, holding a Juicy Juice box in my hand. My heart was beating out of my chest.

"Oh, man," he said, sighing. "Okay."

I couldn't move from where I was standing. I wasn't even sure what I was feeling. It felt like some poisonous combination of shame, loathing, confusion . . .

"Come on, sit down with me, let's talk," Dad said, trying to remain calm. Slowly I peeled myself away from the fridge and closed it behind me, the juice box still in my hand.

"Okay," he said, taking a seat in one of the chairs.

"Why do you keep hiding things from me?" I asked sharply. "You ask me to come down here to see you for the first time in a decade, and watch you get married. Then, when I'm halfway here, you tell me the wedding is off, but I *still* show up, and *somehow* it doesn't seem relevant to tell me—until I'm sitting in your *kitchen*—that you have kids?!"

The juice box burst in my hand. I dropped it, and

immediately started sobbing. My hands flung to my face, hot tears pouring down my cheeks. I doubled over onto the tabletop, my forearms pressing down into where the juice had spilled, my whole body heaving with moans and whimpers. The tears kept coming and coming, like a blown-out fire hydrant pouring into the street. Dad reached across the tabletop and touched my arm. I drew it back and jumped backwards. I stumbled back over to the refrigerator and leaned up against the door.

This is the last place I want to be, I repeated in my head. *Why did I do this to myself? This is a person who doesn't love me—who never loved me! He tricked me into coming here. If I turn and sprint out of this room right now, I won't ever have to look back, and I can be home by tomorrow—*

"I'm so sorry," Dad said softly. He sniffled. I didn't say anything in return. If he thought I would comfort him right now, he was dead wrong. "This wasn't supposed to happen like this," he said sadly. "Not at all. This was supposed to be a happy thing. For us to make a new relationship, as adults. I couldn't bear the thought of going through the rest of my life without you in it. And I wanted you with me as I started a new part of my life. So you'd come down here, see me, meet Teresa, and meet . . . well . . . "

"Your kids," I said softly.

"I should have told you," he said. "I see that now. I just didn't want to scare you off. It seemed like too much all at once."

"I am *this* close to running out of here and never coming back," I said. I turned to face him, staring him dead in the eyes.

He had nothing to say to that. He looked down, ashamed.

"Why aren't you better at this?" I asked, not backing down. "This is your whole master plan, but it feels like I'm the one who has to find things out, who has to ask the questions. I didn't *ask* for any of this!"

"Hey!" he barked. I jumped, shocked at the sudden change in his voice. "I'm struggling here too, Sara. Everything fell apart yesterday—less than twenty-four hours ago, okay? Yesterday we were planning a wedding, and we were getting this big house ready for a reception, and we were putting the finishing touches on the cards for every place setting, and our kids were trying on their dresses again, because they loved them so much. And now . . . " He looked upward to the high ceilings, across the expansive room. Then he looked back at me, and outstretched his arms. "It's all broken."

Now I was the one with nothing to say. Just like earlier that day on the phone, his sadness stopped me in my tracks. He looked very small all of a sudden, sitting in a kitchen—in a house, in a neighborhood— meant for many more than one.

"So can we just talk?" Dad implored me. "Please?"

I took a deep breath. "Yeah," I said firmly. "That'd be good."

He got up, crossed to the fridge, and pulled out two bottles of Shiner Bock beer. "Texas-made," he said, smiling. "Take the edge off."

"I'm not twenty-one," I said. *Of course, he doesn't even know how old I am.*

"And I'm not a cop," Dad said swiftly. I shook my head again, hoping he'd drop it.

"Well, I'll have yours then," he said, opening two beers at once, and seeming to think nothing of it.

He sat back down across the island from me and we just looked at each other. I had no idea where to start. With every second of silence that ticked by, six more questions cropped up in my head. My mouth felt glued shut.

"How's school?" Dad offered.

I stared back at him. "No," I said.

"No?"

"I don't want to start there," I said. "Why'd you leave, Dad?"

He jolted forward at my question, like his chair had suddenly lost a leg. "Uh . . . well . . . "

"You and Mom fought all the time, and you still do. I know."

He rubbed his temples. "Honestly, Sara," he said, "we split up for the same reasons a lot of couples split up. Our relationship couldn't bear the tension and the stress of being parents. Of money being tight, of dinner to be cooked, and laundry to be done. We tried therapy for a few months. I even spent some time in a hotel, to see if that would help, but nothing did."

"But you didn't just 'split up,'" I said. "You *walked out.*"

He met my hard, unswerving gaze. "You're right," he said. "That's exactly right. Walking out on your wife and your kid is the lowest of the low. It was an immature, selfish thing to do. And I will always be sorry I did it."

"So why didn't you come back?" I asked. "If you feel so guilty. It's been twelve years, you know."

"With every passing day, that seemed more and more impossible to do. You know, I didn't actually leave Barrington for two months after I left you and Mom. I drove by the house all the time. One time I even parked the car and had one foot out the door, ready to walk back up to the front porch . . . but I couldn't do it. I got in my car and left. Left Barrington, left Illinois. I kept driving until I got to Texas."

I sighed. This was the first I had ever heard about what actually happened right after he left home. My whole life I'd seen him as a cold-hearted monster, but now . . .

"Mom never told me any of this stuff," I said.

"She doesn't know it," he said, shrugging. "I kept it all to myself. I didn't want to burden you guys with my indecisiveness then, or now."

Is he telling the truth? I wondered. I had no reason to trust a single word that came out of his mouth. I barely knew the guy, after all. "You don't need to sugarcoat anything," I said. "I'd rather hear what really happened."

"What?" he gawked at me, looking hurt. "I'm telling you, Sara, this is what happened. I was selfish, I was cold, and I had no idea what to do with myself afterward. I knew I had already hurt you and Mom so much, I figured the least painful thing I could do would be to just leave and let the two of you move on. Mom and I settled the whole thing with a divorce lawyer remotely and I agreed to pay alimony, and . . . you know all that, I guess."

I drummed my fingers on the table anxiously, resisting feeling bad for him. *He does* not *deserve your pity!* I reminded myself.

He shook his head sadly. "You have no idea the number of plane tickets I've bought back to Chicago," he said. "I even got as far as the gate onto the plane once. But I stayed away."

At this point, I realized, if he was lying, he was a sociopath. I let myself respond honestly. "Whoa."

I sat back in my chair heavily and looked at the gleaming rack of copper pots that hung above our heads. I replayed as many images in my head as I could muster of that warm, crystal-clear summer morning. I'd relived it so many times over my life, feeling the tears on my cheeks, looking upward at my mom, who was trembling with sadness . . . Was that *only* sadness she had been feeling? Maybe it was regret, maybe it was guilt, maybe it was relief. Maybe it was all of the above.

My memory of that morning seemed suddenly

completely wrong. Nothing I thought I knew was right. Watching my dad turn down the front walk carrying his two suitcases—up until now, I watched and rewatched him walk away as a coward, a poor excuse for a father. But for all I knew, my dad had been crying as he walked toward his truck carrying those two suitcases, wondering what else he could have done to save his marriage and his family.

This was all almost too much for me to handle. I felt like I was drowning, just as I did when I first heard Dad's voice on my phone a few days before. All I could do was take deep breaths and try to soak the news in.

"Phew," Dad said, exhaling. "I didn't think I'd ever get to tell you about that."

"I'm glad you did," I said. I took a deep breath and moved onto the next question I needed an answer to.

"Your fiancée," I said. "Who is she?"

"Well, there's one thing she's not," Dad said, "and that's my fiancée. She's a lot of things, but she's not that."

"Oh. Right." I blushed, kicking myself for being

so insensitive. I pushed myself to remember that for every ounce of pain and confusion I was feeling, Dad was feeling that much more. He was remembering how his first marriage ended, while still dealing with the fact that his next chance at a marriage had just crumbled.

"Teresa," he said dryly. "I met her at work, about eight years ago."

"Wait . . . where do you work?" I asked. I realized the list of things I had no answers for was only growing.

"I'm the CFO of an oil company here," he said plainly.

My eyes bulged. "Whoa."

"I got lucky. A guy I used to work with at my consulting firm back in Chicago had come down here and started the company. He owed me one. And since then I've sort of climbed the ladder. Hence . . . " He held out his arms, showing off the picture-perfect kitchen.

I offered a small smile. "Understood. That's impressive."

He shook his head bashfully. "Nah, I got lucky, like I said."

"So, Teresa worked there too?" I asked.

"Yeah," Dad said. "She works in HR. Worked. Works. I don't know. Anyway, she's really good at her job. We started talking, started spending time together—just friends at first. You know how that goes."

What was he getting at? Was this more hinting about my relationship with Pete? I decided not to press the subject.

"Eventually we started dating, but I told her I wasn't ready to settle down anytime soon. This was still five years ago."

"Did you tell her what happened to you and Mom?"

"Not explicitly, but I said I had some skeletons in the closet, and I really wanted to take things slow."

"Seems smart," I said.

"But things don't stay so simple, no matter how much you want them to," Dad said. He stared down at his beer bottle, where his hands were picking at the paper label.

"What?" I asked.

"She got pregnant," he said. "And, uh, lightning struck twice."

"Twins?" I asked. Dad looked back and nodded ever so slightly. I could sense the pain and anguish creeping up inside of him. "Rough."

"Yep, you said it," Dad said. "So we've tried to ease into it. She kept the kids at her place for a few years, and I visited sometimes, enough to get to know them. Then we moved in here a year ago, to give the kids some stability in their lives. Then we thought we should tie the knot, that we had waited long enough, and . . ."

He trailed off, his eyes glistening. Without thinking, I reached across the tabletop and took his hand. I squeezed it and looked at him, hoping to make eye contact and try to tell him I felt sorry for him . . . but he was distant, totally trapped in his own world. We sat like that for a while, me warming up his hand with mine, searching for his eyes.

"Thanks," he said, eventually. "I just keep replaying our last conversation in my head, you know?" He looked back at me, finally, expectantly.

Of course, I wanted to say. *Of course I know that feeling. I've been replaying one very specific memory for as long as I can remember.* But all I said out loud was, "Yeah. Totally."

"I just got cold feet," he said. "I hate that phrase, but there it is. I thought if we waited for a while, until we—I—could really be sure I was ready, then I'd be able to take the plunge. But here we were, the day before, and . . . you know the feeling you have when you wake up in the middle of the night and have to throw up?"

Where was this going? "Yeah," I said hesitantly.

"That's what I'd been having about the wedding. I had regret, I started dreading it—but I ignored it. I told myself everything would be fine. Then it crept up again a few days later. I tried to ignore it. But eventually you just have to go and say, 'This is going to be really unpleasant, but I have to do this if I'm ever going to feel better again.'"

"So what did you do?" I asked.

"I told her I wasn't ready. We were sitting right here. She was going over the final guest list with me, we were looking at the seating plan . . . and I said I didn't want to do it. She tried to reason with me, reassure me, but I put my foot down. I said I'd pay for everything. We would be able to still pay for another ceremony later on . . . but she'd had it. She stormed upstairs and got the kids. She said this was over. She'd held out for too long, and she couldn't waste any more time. In less than half an hour, she was gone."

Those last few words seemed to echo in the giant kitchen, bouncing off the pristine granite countertops. Dad looked back at me, tears rolling down his cheeks.

"I'm so sorry, Dad," I said.

"Don't pity me," he said, "I'm doing enough of that for myself." Then he abruptly stood up, shook his head. "Agh, what are we doing here? We should be celebrating—this is a *reunion!* I'm ruining what should be a fun night!"

"It was never gonna be fun," I said sharply.

Dad took a deep breath and nodded. "Smart kid," he said. "Smart, smart kid. Your mom's done a good job with you."

I waved that comment off like an annoying mosquito. "Have you talked to your kids?" I asked. I liked feeling like I was the powerful one here, that I was the calm and collected adult in the room.

"She hasn't let me," he said. "But she's going to Austin to stay with her parents for a while, and while she's there . . . the kids are going to be with me."

My heart skipped a beat. "They're going to be . . . "

"Here," Dad said. "They're your half-siblings, Sara. Anna and Lily. Cute as can be. And they'll be here in . . . " He looked at his watch. "Twelve hours."

He must have stared at me, waiting for a response, but I was half a world away. This was all starting to be more than I could handle.

I came back to earth when Dad said the only word

that made sense. The only word that made sense in the last four bizarre days.

"Surprised?"

– – –

My heart was pounding as I lay down on the king bed in one of two guest rooms an hour later. The last few days had all been confusing and emotional . . . but this one was the most overwhelming yet. And yet even with everything Dad and I had talked about—how he and my mom came to separate, how he'd met Teresa, what happened yesterday that led them to end their relationship, the fact that I would meet their kids, my half-siblings, in the morning—I felt . . . okay.

Maybe I finally had a dad. Maybe this had been the first of a lot of hard, emotional conversations we'd have, the kind fathers and daughters are supposed to have.

My phone buzzed across the room, and I went to pick it up. A name I had all but forgotten for the last few days shone brightly: Maria Alvarez. *Oh, this will be good,* I thought.

"Hello?" Instantly I was assaulted with a blast of loud, bass-heavy dance music, and what sounded like a thousand people all talking at once.

I could barely hear Maria above the fray. Her voice was all smoky and scratchy, probably from singing all day and partying all night. "Girl!" she screamed.

"Maria, I can barely hear you," I said. "Can you step outside or something? Where even are you?"

"Ugh, fine, hold on." I listened as she moved across what sounded like a very crowded room—I could hear her phone brush up against people's bodies, and the occasional "Watch where you're going!"

Finally, I heard a door slam and the background noise dropped away. "Can you hear me now?" Maria asked. "Ha! Remember, 'Can you hear me now?' Remember that Sara? Sara! Remember? The commercials?"

"Yes," I said. "Got it."

"'Can you hear me now? Buy my cell phone, I'm

a nerd, I have big glasses.' Whatever happened to that guy?"

I giggled. This was exactly what I needed to cap off this crazy, exhausting day. "How are you?" I asked.

"Ugh, Sara, LA is amazing, you need to get here!"

"Are you guys clubbing?"

"No, no," Maria said, "we're at this house party at USC. We're crashing with some other a cappella group at their place."

"Of course," I said. "All you crazy a cappella kids."

"Sara, listen."

"Okay, I'm listening?" I said hesitantly, waiting for a punch line.

"Are you listening?"

"Yes."

"Two words. All male." She cackled loudly, then did her best club air horn. "Bwahhhh, bwah, bwah, bwahhh!"

"I'm thrilled for you," I said, chuckling.

"Nah, but they're all weird-looking kinda, I dunno.

Anyway, what's up with you? You and Pete make out yet?"

Of course this was why she was calling! "No!" I yelled. "Not even close!"

"What?!" she screamed, probably waking up half the neighborhood. "Girl! You have been wasting precious time!"

"That's not happening," I said.

"You are not fooling me, Sara. You're not fooling me, and you're not fooling him, and you're not fooling your dad—oh my God, your dad! What's up with your dad?!"

"Oh, man," I said. "Well, he called off his wedding. Broke *this* woman's heart too. Seems to be good at that."

"What?!" Maria yelled again. By now she had probably woken up every student at USC.

"Crazy, right? And get this, he has kids. Two four-year-old girls. Twins."

"OMG, that's unreal! Sara! You have sisters!"

"I know!" I said, smiling. I was surprising myself.

Finding out about my sisters was shocking, but it hadn't taken long for me to be totally, completely excited to meet them.

"Are they *so* cute?" Maria asked.

"They'll be here tomorrow," I said. "Tomorrow morning."

Maria gushed, suddenly opening up like a broken dam. "I wish I could have you as my older sister, Sara. I really do. They're gonna be so obsessed with you and want to be you and be as smart and as cool and as beautiful and as sophisticated as their older sister. Like . . . it's so obvious to me."

I blushed, my cheeks burning up. "Aw, Maria, that's so—"

"Oh my God, Sara," Maria cut in. "I made out with Tim yesterday!"

"What?!" I yelled. Tim was a senior in her a cappella group and an economics major in the running for valedictorian, who also happened to be an award-winning guitarist and songwriter. "You've wanted that for so long!"

"I know," Maria said proudly.

"Was it everything you wanted?"

"Eh," Maria said dryly. "He had just eaten Chipotle so, like, whatever—but anyway I should go."

"Oh," I said, sad to hear our talk was over so quickly. "Well, it was great to hear from you. I don't know what's gonna happen down here. I still might not have much of a dad when I get home, but I'm glad I'll have you, okay?"

"You're dumb," she said, which I knew was code for *I love you, too.*

"Now go kiss Tim," I said.

She guffawed. "I'll buy him some Listerine this time. Bye, girl!"

I hung up the phone and put it next to me on the mattress. As I drifted off to sleep, I smiled. In spite of everything, I smiled.

Chapter Six

*A*FIRM KNOCK ON THE DOOR RIPPED ME FROM A dream the next morning. I tried to grab onto the strands of the dream before it slipped away. There was a raging thunderstorm, and Pete and I were trapped somewhere together . . . but then it was gone.

"Come in," I said, and Dad immediately entered, clad in plaid pajama pants and a ratty Princeton Crew T-shirt, carrying two mugs of coffee.

"You're up?" he asked quietly.

"I am now," I said, smiling.

"Figured I better start totaling up some dad points,"

he said, indicating the coffee mugs. "I took a wild guess . . . black?"

I smiled, charmed by how hard he was working. I usually put a dash of skim milk and a spoonful of sugar in my coffee, but he didn't have to know that.

"Perfect," I said. "That's nice of you." I sat up and took the mug from him, and he took a seat at the foot of the bed.

"Plus ten dad points!" he said, beaming.

"Is Pete up?" I asked.

"Oh, yeah," Dad said. "He was up before I was. He insisted on making breakfast. Who am I to turn him down, huh? Seems like a really great guy."

I had a momentary impulse to quickly shut down any idea he had that Pete and I were a couple . . . but it passed. I realized, looking at Dad, that he and I had a lot of ground still to cover. *He's still basically a stranger to you, Sara,* I reminded myself.

I took a sip of the piping hot coffee to fill the silence. It was some kind of expensive, trendy roast, both bitter and sour. I smiled through it.

Dad leaned forward and put his hand on my foot. "I just wanted to say how grateful I am for our conversation last night. I had no idea what you'd be like, or what you might want to know, or what you wouldn't want to know. You're a very empathetic person, Sara. I don't know where you got it from, but I am very impressed with you."

"Thank you," I said tentatively.

"My pleasure," Dad said. "I want us to be as honest with each other as possible."

"Breakfast!" came a forceful call from downstairs.

"Ooh, let's go see what he made, huh? I bet you're starved." He leapt off the bed and offered me a hand.

I wasn't at all surprised to see what Pete had created in the kitchen. He was a confident cook and had made all kinds of gourmet meals for our friends over the last year. Of course my dad, like anyone who doesn't know Pete well, was amazed. "Holy crow!" he exclaimed, looking at the spread.

"Well, you haven't tasted any of it yet," Pete said bashfully. He was already dressed for the day, in a handsome navy-blue polo and rust-brown khakis. *Where's the Northwestern gear?* I wondered. *Who's he trying to impress?* He wasn't helping to clarify Dad's confusion about my relationship with Pete. This was just Pete being Pete, not being my boyfriend . . . right?

"So, what have we got here?" Dad asked. He was practically drooling.

Pete smiled and took Dad on a tour through the breakfast he'd made. "Well, I took a look in the fridge and found a few things, I hope that's okay. I made a little fruit salad—strawberries, blueberries, raspberries. And a few bananas on a counter behind a cereal box— at the perfect point of ripeness, I might add. Well done on that front," Pete said.

Dad turned and looked at me, beaming. "I didn't even know we *had* bananas!" he exclaimed.

"Then we've got some scrambled eggs with Gruyère and ricotta, with some spinach, red bell pepper and sautéed onion," Pete continued. He pointed to the steaming platter of eggs and vegetables. The light coming in from the big windows caught the steam rising off the piping hot food. *Pete's outdone himself . . . again.*

"And this?" Dad asked, pointing to a small bowl containing what was obviously yogurt.

"It's yogurt," Pete said. "Greek yogurt with a little honey to cut the sourness."

"Well, plus ten boyfriend points to you, my man," Dad said. He immediately realized his mistake when neither Pete nor I said anything. He stammered, "Er— sorry, I mean . . . me, I say 'boyfriend' the same way you girls call your friends 'girlfriends,' you know . . . "

"No sweat, Danny," Pete said, clapping him on the back. *How long was I asleep?* I wondered. It seemed like while I was dreaming, Pete and Dad had both rushed the same fraternity and were sworn brothers for life.

Pete served up the food and the three of us sat in the dining room to eat. The big windows in the dining room opened onto the house's side yard. A sprawling, perfectly trimmed lawn was scattered with kids' toys, thrown around as if they were disposed of in a hurry.

"Another perfect Texas morning," Dad said, as if reading my mind.

I put a spoonful of yogurt and berries in my mouth and savored the bright, summery flavors. I watched Dad take his first bite as well, and practically double over in ecstasy. He caught me looking at him, and his eyes sprang open like a deer in headlights.

"Do I have yogurt on my chin?" he asked, frantically dabbing his face with a napkin.

"No, no!" I laughed. "You just seem like you're really into that yogurt."

He shrugged his shoulders in a big, cartoonish way. "How could you not be?" With that he put another spoonful in his mouth, and many more after that. In spite of myself, trying to keep my distance, I laughed along with him.

I looked over at Pete. "I talked to Maria last night."

Pete laughed, sensing there might be a funny story coming. "Who's Maria?" Dad asked.

"Her—*our* friend from school," Pete said. "She's out in California with her a cappella group."

"She was having a pretty . . . *fun time*," I said.

"Ah, very cool," Dad said. "You know, I was in an a cappella group in college."

I gawked at him. "Really?"

"Oh, yeah," he said proudly. "The Princeton Monotones."

Pete laughed. "Monotones?"

"We we're all male," Dad said. "Only male voices. Monotones." When we didn't laugh, he muttered, "Ivy League humor, I guess."

"Yeah, it's not great," I said. But still, I smiled. Each new fact I picked up about Dad was like a little gift.

Just then, the doorbell rang, and the same assorted clangs and bongs we had heard last night echoed around the house.

"Aha!" Dad said, getting up from his chair. Immediately my pulse quickened.

"Should I follow you?" I asked, but Dad was already on his way to the front door. I figured I probably shouldn't, but it was either that or stay in the dining room with Pete. I sped off after Dad, waving Pete off as he tried to follow.

I caught up with Dad just as he was opening the massive front door. There stood two little girls, wearing identical blue-and-white-checkered jumpers with white shoes and tall white socks. One of them had her hair up and tied in a classic white bow. They looked like they had just walked out of an American Girl doll catalog.

"Daddy!" they screamed in unison, and charged through the doorway. They each hugged one of Dad's legs and squeezed tight.

"Where'd you go?" one of them demanded, looking up at him.

"Where did I go? Where did *you* go?" Dad retorted, patting her on the head. Both girls giggled. It killed me to hear the barely hidden sadness in his voice.

I looked up from the kids hugging my dad's legs to see who I knew must be Teresa. She was a severe woman wearing a summery knee-length floral dress, pinched together at her slim waist by a red leather belt.

"I take it you're Sara," Teresa said in a thick Texas accent.

"Hi, yep," I said, extending my hand. She held hers out flat, fingers facing the floor, and bent it slightly at the wrist. I was thrown off for a second, and then I realized she wanted me to grasp the ends of her fingers. *What century do you live in?* I wondered.

"I've heard quite a bit about you lately," she said.

"And I, you," I said. "It's nice to meet you."

Hearing my voice, the girls looked up from Dad's legs and gawked at me. I realized it was possible nobody told them I'd even be here, much less who exactly I was.

"I'll be back next Thursday," Teresa said, returning her gaze to my dad. "I'll come get them straight from the airport."

"All right then," Dad said meekly. "We'll be here."

"Be good, girls," Teresa said. "I'll see you soon."

"Bye, Mommy," the twins said. Teresa kissed them both on the head and then was gone. I looked at Dad as he watched Teresa walk away from the house. For the first time that morning, he wasn't smiling. A look of complete defeat hung heavily across his face. But I tried not to pity him too much. *He's doing to Teresa and the girls what he did to you and Mom,* I reminded myself. *He's giving up. He's being selfish.*

But it obviously wasn't that simple. He was plenty torn up inside, and despite all that I couldn't help but feel bad for him.

"Well," Dad said, looking down at the girls, trying to put on a show of happiness for them. "Are you guys hungry?"

"Yeah," the girl wearing a bow said. "Mommy only has yuck food at her house. Tofu!"

"Lima beans!" screamed the other. I laughed. It had been years since I'd spent time with a young kid. Dad ushered the two girls farther into the house, and they took off ahead of him back into the kitchen. I watched all three of them go, and I realized—*really* realized, for the first time—that they were my family. My family had exploded in size in just a few days. What used to be just my mom and me now included a dad and two half-siblings.

This is what family feels like, I said to myself.

My reverie was quickly interrupted by one of the girls piping up again. "Who's that?" She had found Pete.

"That's Sara's friend," Dad said.

"Who's Sara?" one of the girls retorted. Dad and Pete both looked awkward. I slowly walked back towards the kitchen.

"I'm Sara," I said. The girls turned around to face me.

"Girls," Dad said, "this is Sara. She's a new part of our family. Sara, this is Lily," he said, pointing to the girl with a bow in her hair. "And this is Anna."

"Nice to meet you," I said, waving.

"What do you mean she's in our family?" Lily asked, still staring straight at me. She put her hands on her hips like a skeptical old woman.

"It's a little complicated," Dad said. "Why don't we get you guys some food first?"

Over a second round of breakfast, Dad laid everything out as clearly as he could. He explained that I had lived with him when I was the girls' age, and how for an unhappy reason I hadn't seen him since then. But that if things went well, I would be around a lot more now.

"Sara is my daughter, just like you are both my daughters," Dad said. The girls' eyes widened.

Then, Lily managed to utter, "Her?"

"Yes, her," I said, before correcting myself. "Me. I'm your sister. Anna's your sister, and I'm your sister, too. Only we have different mommies. We have the same dad." I looked over at Dad and smiled.

"I'm the odd one out," Pete said, chuckling. I had almost forgotten he was there. "You're not related to me!"

"You have red hair," Anna offered.

"Honey, that's rude," Dad said.

"Why? He does!" Lily retorted.

"Red hair is fine to have," he said quietly. "It's perfectly normal." He weirdly made eye contact with Pete. "Perfectly normal thing to have red hair." Pete forced a smile back, obviously confused as to why his hair needed so much defending.

All in all, the girls dealt with the confusion much better than I guessed they would. They didn't seem to really understand the entire situation—after all, they weren't even clear on how babies get made in the first place—but they accepted it.

Once the girls got a grasp of who Pete and I were, they moved on. "What are we doing today, Daddy?" Lily asked.

Lily and I had the same thought. "It's such a perfect day," I said excitedly. "And neither Pete nor I have been here before, obviously, so maybe you guys could show us around town, or something?" I looked at the girls, a cheery smile spread out on my face. "Where do you guys like to go on beautiful summer days?"

"Well, gosh," Dad said, his tone distinctly darker than mine. "Sorry to be *that* guy, but I *will* have to go into work today. But of course you all can do something fun!" I looked over at him, my gaze hardening.

Wait a second, did you not have this day off from work? I grumbled in my head. *Hadn't you planned to be at the altar this very moment?*

"Again?!" Anna groaned. "You always have boring work!"

I wondered then if he spent a lot of time at the office, away from the family. I wondered if that might have been part of the problem.

Suddenly my thoughts spun out of control. *Maybe he hasn't changed a bit since he left me and Mom behind. Maybe he's just as distant and checked-out and selfish as he always was! And here I was pitying him for bailing on his fiancée and their daughters. Selfish jerk!*

"Just for a bit, I promise," he said. "Girls, you can come with me, or not. I bet these two could be fun to hang out with for a while." Then Dad quickly glanced up at me. "If they'd be interested, of course."

I didn't say anything, as I was trapped in my head, cursing myself for letting him off the hook so easily.

Pete piped up, "Well, I can't speak for Sara, but I'm a great babysitter."

"We're not babies!" Lily yelled. "We're four and four-sixths!"

"Oh, excuse me then," said Pete, smiling. "So who are you planning on voting for in the next election?"

Anna looked at Pete, then at me, then at her dad. "What?" she asked.

Dad chuckled. "You're very mature for your age, he's saying." Anna smiled contentedly.

It was all too easy to imagine the scheme Dad was constructing. He wasn't interested in being a father to anyone—me, Lily, or Anna—or a husband to either Mom or Teresa. And he had manipulated Pete and me into his web again, only to serve as substitute parents while he acted on his own behalf. *Once a bad parent, always a bad parent.*

Lily jumped down from her chair at the table and walked over to Dad, climbing onto his lap. "When is the wedding, Daddy?" Lily asked.

The room fell silent. My heart slammed against my

chest. Had they not told them? Did these poor kids still think they were finally getting a united home?

"Is it today?" Anna asked. "Or tomorrow?"

"Ooh! Can we try on our dresses again?" Lily squealed. "I like the big bow on mine!"

"And our fancy shoes!"

"And—"

"*Girls,*" Dad said sternly. Lily and Anna stopped their giggling immediately and stared at him, their faces each a shade whiter. "I'm sorry. I'm not angry. I'm just . . . " He faded away. He didn't have the words. "It's not happening, girls. Did Mommy not tell you?"

Now it was the girls' turn to fall silent. They looked at each other, just like two adults do when they're completely at a loss. It wasn't that they didn't understand, it was that they couldn't believe it.

"I'm sorry, kids," Dad said. "I know how excited you were. But Mommy and I realized we weren't ready."

Is that really the truth? I wondered. I looked over

at Pete, who was watching the entire proceedings in silence. I was back at square one with him, like the previous day hadn't happened. Dad felt like a complete stranger to me again.

"Will we still live here?" Lily asked. I gritted my teeth. When I left home, I thought I was going to a wedding, where I would try to get to know my estranged father. But now, here I was, watching him alienate his *other* daughters, just like he did to me. *Great.*

– – –

Half an hour later, after a marathon session of questions the girls raised about their parents' breakup, Lily and Anna were seated on the couch, silently watching an episode of *Doc McStuffins*. Pete nobly sat with them. Even Pete wasn't sure how to handle the emotions of the situation, so he sat quietly and perfectly still. Like he was trying to vanish into thin air.

In the kitchen, Dad and I silently cleaned up the

rest of the breakfast. I rinsed dishes in the sink. He put a few things in Tupperware and placed them back in the fridge. I wondered if he wanted me to say something, or if he just wanted company. We'd been at it for a full ten minutes before anybody said anything.

"Something big came up at work," he finally said, his back to me. "I'm sorry. I wish I could get out of it, but . . ."

I scrubbed the egg pan, hesitant to open my mouth for fear of saying something irresponsible.

"Sara?" he asked timidly.

"I heard you," I said darkly. I wasn't going to let him get away with manipulating me anymore.

"I get it, you're mad," he said. "I am too. Trust me, it's my last choice for how to spend this day."

I took a deep breath, standing up straight from the sink. *Fighting can only get you so far,* I mused. *He has to go to work. The question is what you're going to do about it.*

"I guess this way I can get to know my half-sisters a little easier," I said, trying to find some silver lining.

"There you go," he said. "Probably the less you see of me, the better."

I turned to look at him, stone-faced. "When do you need to go?"

His blank look told me that he needed to go ASAP. *You barely know me,* I thought. *Why are you okay leaving your kids with me and a total stranger?*

He looked more anxious by the second. Even though I still wasn't sure why he was even considering it, I knew I was up to it. I wasn't sure Dad was worth my time, but my sweet, adorable half-sisters definitely were. "Okay," I said, "I can handle it."

"I really appreciate it, Sara," he said, rinsing the last plate and putting it in the drying rack. "Let's go tell the girls."

In the living room, the girls' show was still playing on the TV, but nobody was watching. Instead, Lily and Anna were enthralled with Pete, asking him questions and staring at him wide-eyed and expectant.

"Does it snow all the time in Chicago?" Lily asked.

"No, not at all," Pete said. "Last summer it was

like the Amazon rain forest outside. You walk out of your house and immediately you start sweating!" He was acting like I'd never seen him. His face was overly expressive, his smile wide, his gestures big and broad. The girls giggled happily, hanging on every word.

"It snowed once in Texas," Anna said.

"One time *ever?*" Pete asked.

"Yeah!" Lily said. "It happened right outside!"

"I'm glad you guys made a new friend," Dad said, putting his hands on his hips.

Lily turned around to look at him. "Yeah, this is Pete, he's funny! He's funny like a clown."

"And he has red hair like a clown!" Anna bellowed. The girls cracked up, falling all over the couch and each other.

"How'd you feel about hanging out with Pete and Sara for a while?" Dad asked. The girls' eyes lit up—and they looked back to their new best friend Pete. I wasn't sure they even remembered I was there.

– – –

An hour later, I was in yet another place I never thought I'd be, behind the wheel of my dad's Chevy Suburban ("a Texas-sized ride," he'd said), with Pete beside me and two small girls in the backseat. Dad insisted he take my car and I take his, so that the girls could watch a DVD on the seatback screens they depended on.

"You should have to be certified to drive this thing," I said. It felt like sitting behind the wheel of a school bus.

"Can we go?!" whined Lily from the backseat.

"Yep, okay," I said, on edge. "You're navigating, right?" I asked Pete.

"Got it right here. Only twenty-three minutes to the Wild Western Mall."

"The mall!" screamed Lily from the backseat.

"Can we go on the Ferris wheel?" Anna bellowed. "And get cotton candy? And go to the American Girl store?"

"We'll see," I said dryly. *It's like a mall and an*

amusement park rolled into one, Dad had said. *Perfect for kids, torture for adults.*

After doing a few practice turns around the cul-de-sacs and broad streets of their neighborhood, I felt slightly comfortable behind the wheel of the giant SUV. I knew the drive to the mall included about ten miles on the highway, which I was not looking forward to.

"Where are we going?" asked Lily.

"Yeah, this is the wrong way," Anna said.

Pete chuckled. "Smart kids! If you're so smart, how about you tell us how to get there? You've been there before. We haven't."

Pete's chipper attitude was starting to wear on me. Why did he have to pretend everything was okay? I just wanted these few hours to be over with, for my dad to get back home so I could talk to him just like I did the night before. There were countless questions I still had for him, so much ground yet to cover.

"Okay!" the girls said in unison. "Turn right!" Pete

looked over at me, smiling broadly. I sighed and tried to resist putting the kibosh on the whole trip.

"Okeydokey," I said, with an edge to my voice. "A right turn it is."

Surprisingly, the girls managed to get us most of the way there—at least, until we were on the freeway and looking for our exit. Landmarks were scarce out there. It was classic suburban sprawl, the land littered with homes that looked completely identical. They looked like they had dropped down from the sky all at the same moment, landing in perfect order.

"What do you think? Creekside Lane, or Lyndon B. Johnson Parkway?" Pete asked. There was no response. The kids had grown bored with the "find the mall" game and were sucked back into their screens.

"Well, it was good while it lasted," Pete muttered. The car fell silent for a while.

"So . . . which is it?" I asked eventually. "I *do* need to get off sometime."

"Oh," Pete said. "It's LBJ Parkway. Sorry."

I shook my head and smiled tightly in his direction, as if to say, *Don't worry about it.*

Pete's expression hardened a bit. "Are you okay?" he whispered.

Took you long enough to notice, I thought grimly. "Fine," I managed. "Just a little tired."

"Yeah."

I said nothing, offered him no thanks for asking. Then, obviously getting a little desperate, Pete reached over and placed his hand on mine, on top of the steering wheel.

"Whoa!" I said, unable to control myself. I sharply snapped my hand away. "Whoa! Pete, don't do that! Driving this stupid thing is hard enough as it is!"

Taken aback, Pete uttered a sharp, "Oh," and flopped his hand into his lap. I could tell his head was swimming, wondering where he went wrong. I knew I owed him an explanation for why I was suddenly so cranky—it was Dad's fault, not his—but I decided not to risk having the girls overhear. I gave Pete a curt smile but he didn't notice. His gaze was focused hard out the window.

Somehow I steered the giant SUV all the way to the mall, and my temples throbbed at the mere sight of it. It was an endless, hulking structure. Broad groups of big-boned Texas families strolled across the steamy parking lot. They all looked positively blissful, ready to shop and play and eat.

I pushed my head back against the headrest, groaning. *How long do I have to put up with this?*

– – –

The Wild Western lived up to Dad's description all too well. The amusement park sat directly in the middle of the mall, the eye of the hurricane. It was three stories high, crowned by a glass roof that let in the cloudless sky. But the air conditioning was kept at an arctic level. It was so cold I immediately wished I had brought sweatpants and a sweatshirt, as opposed to my denim shorts and tank top.

I was granted a little relief when Pete took the girls on the giant Ferris wheel. I stood at the exit, holding the twins' half-full Icees, staring upward, trying to find the trio among the many swaying compartments.

"Sara!" came Pete's voice from above. I searched around the Ferris wheel, looking for his waving hand.

"Sara!" he called again. Then I spotted him waving frantically toward me, with the girls screaming happily on either side of him. They were swinging around towards the bottom of the wheel, only about fifty feet from where I stood. I forced a grin and waved toward them, still holding the sweating Icees.

"Take a picture!" Pete bellowed.

"I can't!" I said, gesturing with the drinks.

"What?" Pete yelled back.

"I can't take your picture!" I barked. "I'm holding all this crap."

Pete heard me. He just shook his head, bemused. He sat back and told the girls to do the same. They looked up at him, disappointed.

My phone buzzed in my back pocket, startling me. I set the cups at my feet and put my phone to my ear.

"Hello?"

"Hey Sara," came Dad's voice from the other end.

"Hey," I said, relieved to talk to anyone other than Pete or the kids.

"How're things?"

"Things are fine," I said. "They're on the Ferris wheel, I'm . . . supposed to be taking pictures, I guess."

"You're a trooper," he said.

I paused, wondering what was coming next. *He can't have just called to tell me how great I am.*

"So, listen," he said.

"Yeah?" My heart kicked up a couple beats.

"Things are really hectic down here," he said. "Way crazier than I thought they would be. I'm gonna have to be here a while."

My stomach sank. *Are you kidding me right now?!* I wanted to scream. Instead, I managed a quiet, "How long?"

"At least midnight," he said. "Maybe later."

"*Really?!*" I spat, before I could stop myself. I was irritated, I couldn't hide it. This wasn't exactly why I made this trip down here. *I could babysit at home, and be paid for it.*

"I know," he said. "I'm really sorry, Sara. I can't thank you enough for covering for me. Obviously *none* of this was part of the plan."

"Yeah, no duh."

He sighed. "How can I make this up to you?"

I looked toward the Ferris wheel and saw Pete and the girls were walking towards the exit, and towards me. "I have to go," I said tersely. "Just let me know when you'll be home."

I hung up the call without waiting to hear whatever he had to say next.

"Hey, sourpuss," said Pete as he walked up to me.

"Sourpuss! Sourpuss!" the girls chanted in unison. They took the Icees off the floor by my feet.

"I had blue!" Lily shrieked, picking up a cup.

"No, *I* had blue!" Anna screamed in return, trying to wrest the cup from her sister's sticky hands.

"Anna, look at Lily's mouth," Pete said evenly. Anna did, and so did I. Her tongue, teeth, and cheeks were antifreeze-blue.

"Okayyyy," Anna said, picking up her red Icee.

"Who was that on the phone?" Pete asked.

"It was Dad," I said. The girls looked up at me, their eyes wide. "He has to stay at the office awhile longer I guess. So . . . "

"*Party time!*" Pete cheered. The girls giggled and jumped up and down. I wanted to slap him. Again, it was like he was showing off. For whom?

"Can we stay up until he gets home?" Lily asked.

"I don't think so," I said, trying to nip that idea in the bud. "He might not be home until late."

"Sourpuss! Sourpuss!" the girls chanted again.

"Where to next?" Pete asked the girls, trying to pull the focus off of me.

"American Girl dolls!" they cheered together. Pete gazed over to me expectantly.

"It's not my thing either," I said to him dryly. It was

not a smart thing to say. The girls' jaws dropped like I had just uttered every swear word known to mankind.

"What?" Anna asked sadly.

"You don't like American Girl?" Lily said, her eyes as wide as saucers.

"I don't . . . " I stammered. "I just . . . I don't know anything about it!"

Anna smiled broadly. "Oh! We'll teach you!"

And with that, we were off, charging towards another corner of the mall. The girls knew the way all too well, and they sped off ahead of us, weaving among the shoppers. Pete and I walked as fast as we could behind them, just barely keeping an eye on them amid the crush.

Eventually we found our way into the store, and though the girls only beat us inside by about ten seconds, we found them chatting with other girls their age. Like adults over cocktails, they seemed to be comparing notes about their particular dolls. I couldn't help but shake my head in amazement. The store was massive. It covered two sprawling floors, the shelves packed with dolls and miniature clothes and books and so much else. At least a hundred girls of all ages led their frantic families around the aisles and displays— desperately pleading to buy it *all*, I was sure.

Pete and I, still silent, trailed behind Lily and Anna as they walked the aisles. Together with a few new friends, they made their way over to a TV that was playing one of the American Girl movies. Luckily, there were a few open seats, and the girls immediately plopped down to watch, enthralled. *Hopefully it just started,* I thought.

As Pete and I stood there silently, I realized this was my opportunity to let him know why I had been such a pain for the last hour. "Hey," I said, "can we talk?"

He nodded, obviously a little nervous. I gestured toward a corner of the store on the other side of a bookshelf. We walked over to the corner and I made sure I could keep an eye on the girls around the shelf. After I made sure they were still watching the movie, I turned to Pete.

"Hey, so," I started. "I know I've been pretty testy

here for the last couple hours—back at home, in the car, here at the mall . . . ”

“You can say that again,” Pete said, chuckling. But his smile faded when he noticed that I wasn’t playing along.

“Why do you keep doing that?” I said, a little too harshly. If I had thought for one more second, I wouldn’t have asked the question.

Pete stammered. “I . . . well, I’m just trying to, you know, help . . . ”

“By what? You don’t need to be—” But I cut myself off, because I was coming close to flying off the handle at Pete, and he wasn’t even the problem. “Sorry,” I said, rubbing my eyes and taking a deep breath. “I’m just angry with my dad. It’s really nothing about you, and I’m sorry I’m taking it out on you.”

Pete smiled, obviously relieved to hear he wasn’t the problem. “Hey,” he said, shrugging, “that’s what I’m here for.”

“No, it’s not,” I said. “You are not here to be my punching bag.”

Pete smiled but said nothing. Suddenly his face was flush with anxiety and his eyes looked wildly from floor to ceiling. "Well, I'm glad you wanted to talk, actually," he started. "Because . . . "

What is he about to say? I panicked. The only other time I had seen Pete so suddenly anxious was when the barista at the Starbucks in Evanston told him they were out of blueberry muffins, and asked him if he'd rather have banana or chocolate chip.

"Sara," he started haltingly, "I'm so glad you asked me to come down here with you." He paused and I stayed silent, waiting for more. I tucked a strand of my wispy hair behind my ear nervously. "I know this has been such a hard time for you, and I want to be there for you however I can." He took another deep breath. "Sara, I know you probably think of me as just a friend—and don't get me wrong, I really like being your friend, but . . . "

Oh, God. No, he can't be doing this!

He gulped and took a step toward me, reaching his hands out to mine. "Sara, I've loved you since the moment I met you, and I just had to say something, because . . . "

I slapped his hands away with my own, backing away, in a panic. "Whoa, Pete, I . . . " I turned away from him, my face burning. *Why did you have to do this now? You idiot!*

"Oh, gosh, sorry," I heard Pete mumble from behind me. Part of me wanted to comfort him—who doesn't want to comfort their best friend when they're in agony?—but I knew I couldn't do that without making him think I loved him, too. *Which I definitely, definitely do not.*

With my back to Pete, my eyes spun wildly, searching the ceiling and the floor for answers as my face burned. My eyes darted over toward where the girls were sitting, and—

They weren't sitting there anymore. They weren't sitting anywhere.

They were gone.

Chapter Seven

"Oh no," I said under my breath. I brushed past Pete and walked over to the area around the TV. Lily and Anna were nowhere in sight.

"Uh oh," Pete said, coming up behind me.

"Did you see where they went?" I asked.

Instead of answering my question, Pete started, "Hey, can we just—"

"Later," I said sternly. "I really, really can't right now." I sped off to a corner of the store. "Go that way!" I yelled back at Pete. He nodded and turned off away from me, his gaze lingering just slightly in a desperate apology.

I frantically searched the aisles of the store, stopping every few seconds because many of the kids were the girls' height—but I was wrong. Over and over again, I was wrong.

After I had made a lap around the first level of the store, I bounded up the stairs, but Pete was standing there to greet me. He was white as a sheet. "Nothing," he said.

"Oh my God," I said, my stomach churning. "Great. Just great."

"What do we do now?" Pete asked.

"They can't have gone far," I said sternly. "Keep your phone on. Let's split up."

We bounded down the stairs toward the exit. "What are their other favorite stores here?" Pete asked. "Any ideas?"

"I literally just met them, Pete," I said. "The exact same moment you did."

"So—"

"No," I said. We had reached the exit. "Okay, you go left. I'll go right." I sped off.

Soon after I left the American Girl store, I realized how impossible this task seemed. The mall was *huge,* and I had no idea where anything was.

I passed by the Sharper Image, slowing down to peer inside and make sure they weren't playing in the massage chairs. Nothing. I charged onward, passing by a Men's Wearhouse. I blew past it, but immediately realized they *could* be in there—maybe they were hiding in the tie racks? Maybe they'd found one of the fitting rooms and were hiding out inside?

They could literally be anywhere.

I jogged over to a directory of every store in the mall. I scanned it, looking for places kids might be drawn to. Since the girls knew the layout of the mall like the backs of their hands, it wasn't impossible they could have taken off for somewhere far away.

I read the list of stores frantically—Apple, Nike, Bath & Body Works—then it leapt out at me: Disney. That had to be it. And it wasn't far! I sped off again, more of a pop in my step.

As I hustled towards an escalator to the third floor, I

silently cursed all the men in my life—none of whom, apparently, could be trusted. *Dad manipulated and used me, just like both of his wives. Pete thought this was the perfect moment to completely blindside me with—*

I couldn't even finish the thought in my head. It made my stomach twist into a thousand knots. Pete knew how I felt about Anthony Troy. *That* was the kind of guy for me. He was taller, broader, deeper-voiced than Pete. So why did he have to go and make this so complicated? Why put that on me? Especially *now?*

Was anybody on my side?

Suddenly the Disney Store—or, what used to be the Disney Store—appeared in front of me. Rather than a brightly lit expanse accompanied by cheery *Mary Poppins* tunes, all that greeted me was a wall of plywood and a big sign that read, "We'll miss you, Wild Western! Thanks for 17 great years!" Mickey's cheerful face sat next to the sign, really twisting the knife.

I felt completely out of options. My legs, after pushing me onward for the last ten minutes, were trembling. My upper lip soon followed suit, and my eyes burned, welling up. I wasn't even sad, just frustrated. At Pete, at this mall, at these irresponsible and ill-behaved little girls, at Dad for abandoning me here—just like he had abandoned me so many years ago.

I slumped down against the plywood wall, right beneath Mickey. I took out my phone and hopelessly called Pete.

"Hello?" he said softly.

I asked the question, but I already knew the answer. "You found them?"

"No," he said. "I take it you haven't either?"

"*Argh!*" I bellowed, barely restraining myself from tossing my phone down the carpeted hallway.

"What should we do?" Pete asked weakly.

"I have no idea."

"I'm so sorry," Pete said.

"About what?" I asked bitterly. *About your ill-timed declaration of love for me?* I wondered. *About ruining our friendship?*

"I should have watched them more carefully," he said.

I couldn't help but laugh sharply, wiping tears from my cheeks. "Great," I said. I hung up.

I quickly scrolled through my contacts, and called Dad's number. It rang once . . . twice . . . three times . . . and went to voicemail. I swore bitterly in my head, and tried again. Nothing.

Deciding a voicemail was better than nothing, I left a short message. "Hey Dad, it's Sara, call me back as soon as you get this, thanks."

Feeling deflated, I got back up and started walking towards another directory ahead of me. I wasn't hopeful. Nothing had stuck out to me on the list as a particularly kid-friendly place, other than the Disney Store.

Then a different idea sparked to life in my head. I pulled out my phone and Googled Dad's business, Jackson-Flowers Industries. I quickly found a phone number, and dialed.

"Jackson-Flowers Industries," answered a cheery young man's voice, "how can I help you?"

"Hi, this is Sara Jackson," I said quickly. "I'm calling for my dad, Danny? It's urgent."

"Oh. Uh . . . " the man seemed flustered.

"Danny Jackson," I said again, sternly. "The CFO?"

"Here, let me transfer you to . . . " he trailed off.

A woman's voice picked up quickly. "Is this Danny's daughter?" she demanded.

"Yeah, I need to talk to my dad, tell him it's—"

"It's great you called," the woman said. "We've been looking for him all day."

I felt like someone had slapped me in the face, hard. It took me awhile to recover from what the woman had just said—so long that she hesitantly made sure I was there. "Miss?" she asked. "Did you hear what I said?"

"He's . . . he's not there?" I managed.

"Right," she said, sounding impatient. "And it's extremely busy down here. Tell him we need him right away."

"I'm not with him!" I barked. "*I'm* looking for *him!*"

"Well, I don't know what to tell you," the woman said. "I hope you find him. Selfish little brat." Then she promptly hung up.

Now I *did* drop my phone—just like I did when Dad had first called me. Unconsciously my hands flew to the top of my head and pulled my hair right at the roots. I ground my teeth together and wished to go back to that sunny day on the lake. I would do everything differently. I would hang up on him, and never think about him again.

Where could he be? He wasn't with me, he wasn't at home, and he wasn't at work . . . *Is this the real Danny Jackson?* I asked myself. *A liar?*

I could barely get my feet to move, but I knew I had to. I still had this liar's daughters to find, and they were innocent in all of this.

As soon as I got to my feet, my phone rang—was it Dad?

No, it was Pete. My heart skipped a beat—it was beyond time for some good news. "Hello?"

"I'm at the customer service desk," Pete said flatly.

"I told them the girls are missing. They're radioing all the security guards and they're going to make an announcement on the PA system. Just come meet me down here. There's nothing else for us to do."

"Okay," I said. "I'll be there." I hung up, and looked on the nearby directory for the office.

Just then, a stern male voice came over the intercom. "Lily and Anna Jackson, please report to the security office, or find a guard in a blue uniform. Again, Lily and Anna Jackson, please report to a nearby guard, or to the security office. Thank you." That was it. No urgency at all. If the girls hadn't been listening carefully, they almost certainly wouldn't have heard it. I had no hope left.

I needed a distraction while we waited or I was going to drive myself crazy. So as I walked to the security office I called the only person who could be a total breath of fresh air.

"Hey, girl," came Maria's haggard voice from the other end. "What's shakin'?"

"Wow, you don't sound good," I said, chuckling.

Just hearing four words out of her mouth made me smile, and made me miss her more than I was prepared for.

"Yeah, a long night plus a three-hour gig this morning where I sang the same Jessie J song eight times. *No bueno.*"

"I'm sorry but I don't have long to talk," I said.

"Okay?" she asked, concern flooding into her voice.

"So, it's a long story, but right now I'm at a mall in Texas with my two half-sisters."

"OMG! Are they *so* cute?"

"Sort of," I said. "They're little monsters, honestly. But here's the big thing, Pete and I were talking just now . . . and *please* don't say 'I told you so.' But . . . he told me he's in love with me?"

An eternity passed after the words left my mouth. I was almost sure the call had been dropped when Maria laughed on the other end of the line, a booming, earth-shattering cackle. Finally, she found words again, and bellowed, "No he didn't!"

"Yes he did!" I said, laughing in spite of myself. "He

was like, 'Sara, I've loved you since the moment I met you.'"

"Whoa," Maria said with a little chuckle. "So what'd you say?"

"I, like . . . I don't even really know," I said. "He, like, reached out to touch me and I think I . . . slapped his hands away?"

Maria groaned. "What? Come on!"

"I know, I know. It was just like instinctual, you know? I was so overwhelmed! I don't even remember saying anything, I think I just like turned away from him."

"Wait so are you like still standing next to him right now? Why are you calling me? Why aren't you ring-shopping at this mall?"

I couldn't even laugh about that one. "We're not together because right after that happened, I realized Lily and Anna had run away while we weren't looking and now I'm like frantically searching this giant mall for them."

Maria groaned. "So, things are going well for you!"

"You could say so, yeah," I said. "Anyway I don't really know why I called, and I'm gonna have to hang up soon, because Pete's in the security office waiting for the mall cops to bring the girls back. I just wanted to tell somebody, I guess."

"So, why are you so upset about it?" Maria asked, ignoring the fact that I would need to hang up soon.

"What do you mean?"

"Is it the fact that he said he loves you? Or the timing?"

"Both!" I said. "Definitely both."

"Well, he definitely didn't time it right," Maria said. "But honestly, I think you're blowing this a little out of proportion."

"What?!" I yelled. I couldn't believe what I was hearing.

"I know it seems like a big deal," she said, "but this happens between friends. Things get confusing when it's a guy and a girl. You guys really care about each other, right?"

"I guess," I mumbled.

"Of course you do. So you just need to have a talk and get on the same page again. Honestly, it's good he told you, because if he didn't—"

"You have *got* to be kidding me!" I yelled, power-walking across the first floor of the mall towards the security office in the distance. "You, too? God, can't I get anybody to give me a lifeline here?"

Maria spoke quietly. "Sara, come on, I'm just telling you—"

"Sorry, I have to go," I said, hanging up. I shoved my phone back in my pocket without another thought.

When I found Pete inside the security office, I gasped. I had never seen him look so hopeless, so pathetic.

"Hey," I said softly, sidling up to him.

"Hey," he said, avoiding eye contact.

"You're Sara?" asked the sleepy-eyed guard behind the desk.

"Yes," I said. "I'm their half-sister. Will this work?"

"We always find 'em," she said. "Don't you worry."

I took a deep breath, trying to relax. "Okay. If you say so."

"Nothing to do but wait. Have a seat."

Both Pete and I sat in the rigid plastic chairs. Tacky smooth jazz was playing on the speakers in the room, probably to calm anxious parents and guardians just like us. We sat stone-faced and silent for what felt like hours, looking blankly at the desk in front of us. A cheesy, faded poster hung on the opposite wall: a friendly mall cop standing next to two white kids in brightly colored polos. The big, cartoonish text around them read, "Safety! It's always on sale!"

Just then, the sleepy-eyed cop's walkie-talkie crackled to life. "Found 'em, boss," came a young woman's voice.

I practically leapt out of my chair and so did Pete. My heart was going to beat out of my chest. The cop slowly picked up her radio. "The Jackson girls?" she asked.

"That's them, sir," she said. "Bringing them to you now. The parents there?"

The cop eyed us, skeptically. "Half-sister and . . . " She gazed at Pete, evaluating him. "Friend."

There was murmuring on the other end of the radio. I heard a little girl's voice. Then the security guard again. "Yep, they say that sounds right. Just making sure."

"Good job, Martinez," the guard said. "We'll see you soon."

Pete and I sighed and looked at each other. I gave him a half smile. "I was ready to give up! Thank you." I meant it sincerely, but I didn't want to make him think I'd changed my mind about what he'd told me.

Again, we were out of words to say to each other. We had to have a big talk, I knew, but this was definitely not the place to have it. I looked straight ahead at the same dumb poster and willed the girls to get back to the office as fast as humanly possible.

My phone buzzed in my pocket. I took it out, grateful for the distraction. It was a text from . . . Pete? I looked at him next to me quizzically. He met my eyes and nodded back at my phone, imploring me to read what he had sent. I opened the text.

Sorry about that, crappy timing. Can we talk later? I feel like there's more to say.

I locked my phone and put it back in my pocket. I looked at Pete for half a second but I couldn't hold the eye contact. He looked completely devastated, and in spite of myself, it hurt to see him that way.

I heard Maria's words echo through my skull. *I know it seems like a big deal, but this happens between friends. Things get confusing when it's a guy and a girl.*

So he's just confused, I thought to myself. *He thinks he loves me, but what he's just feeling is the love that friends feel—not romantic love.* Was that it?

It's not like you're the world's expert on romantic love, I said to myself, *seeing as you've never had a boyfriend.*

But you know it when you feel it, right? I wondered. I tried to distract myself from continuing the argument raging on inside my head, but the boring office and the dreadful music made it difficult.

Finally, I heard two voices pipe up from outside the

door. Lily and Anna were back, being led inside the door by a young cop, who must have been Martinez. The girls looked completely chill about the fact that they had been separated from their guardians in this giant crowded mall. *I guess it's hard to feel totally alone when you have your sister next to you,* I thought.

I jumped up from my seat and hugged the girls. "Where did you guys go?" I asked urgently, squeezing their small, soft bodies.

"Barnes & Noble!" Lily crowed.

"Yeah, we always go there after American Girl," Anna said matter-of-factly. "Then TCBY, then home."

"Oh," I said, smiling. I pulled back from the hug and looked at them sternly, trying to convey some sense of authority. "I wish you had told me that. We didn't know about your favorite stores. You have to tell me those things, okay?"

Lily and Anna nodded solemnly. I sighed. "Well, I'm just glad to see you again."

Lily looked behind me and beamed. "Pete your hair got even redder!" She cackled, and Anna marched over to inspect Pete's hair. I rubbed my temples, having almost succeeded in forgetting Pete was there. Looking at him, charmed all over again by Lily and Anna, broke my heart. He was a nice guy, he was my friend. But he had made a big mistake. Would we ever be okay again?

But that question was suddenly erased as a much more urgent thought exploded in my head. *Dad. Where's Dad?*

Chapter Eight

TEN MINUTES LATER WE WERE BACK IN THE Suburban hurtling towards home. I couldn't put the Wild Western Mall in the rearview mirror fast enough. It would forever be filled with bad memories for me—of potentially losing my best friend, and actually losing my two young sisters. Never again.

A *Spongebob* DVD was playing quietly in the backseat of the car, but the girls weren't listening to it. They had promptly passed out after I started the engine. I was grateful for it—just to have some peace, but also to think about what we were going to do next. I had told Pete about my conversation with Dad's colleague, and about the confusing and scary situation we were in. I wasn't ready to talk with Pete about anything else, but I knew I needed his help in tracking Dad down.

"Maybe he has two offices?" Pete whispered.

Fighting the late-afternoon glare coming through the windshield, I shook my head. "Even if that were the case, that woman I talked to would know he was there. As far as I can tell, he was telling the truth about just two things. One, that he is actually important at the company. And two, that something major *is* happening there. I don't know what exactly it is, but the woman I talked to sounded totally frantic. Like they couldn't do anything without him."

Pete slumped in his seat. "Man."

"I'm just worried he's not safe. Like, what if he got in an accident or something?" I said.

"But that doesn't make sense," Pete said. "He called you saying that he'd already been at work, and needed to stay longer. Right?"

"Right," I said. "I know. But maybe . . . maybe he

was lying about going to work the first time, but then he actually meant to go, and . . . "

Pete looked over at me, sadly. He didn't have to say anything.

"I know," I said. "I just can't believe he'd lie to me like that! I just met him, I know, but he seems like a pretty decent guy, and he's just trying to do the right thing. Right?"

Pete said nothing, but looked back at the girls. They were still sound asleep. "What should we do about them?"

"We can't tell them," I said. "I mean, what would we say? 'Your dad's been feeding us a pack of lies all day and we don't know where he is'?"

"But at some point—"

"No, we'll just have to track him down before too long. We told them he'd be working late. If we get him home sometime tonight, they won't know any different."

Pete fell silent for a few minutes. "I don't know how I'd be handling this if I were you."

I shuddered. Any comment from him that tiptoed back toward "I love you" territory made me queasy. I stared straight ahead at the road and said nothing.

– – –

Back at the house half an hour later, Pete and I sat in the kitchen while the girls played in the basement.

"All right, so you called him twice—when?" Pete asked.

"Two forty-one."

"And you left a voicemail."

"Yeah, but there's no way to know if he listened to it—"

"Are you sure there's not a way?"

I handed Pete my phone and sighed. "Go ahead, MacGyver." Pete took it and scrolled through a few things, looking at the screen intensely. But he gave up as quickly as he started.

"Yeah, I don't know," he said.

Suddenly, I had an idea. "Give me my phone," I said quickly. Pete handed it to me, his eyes wide.

"What are you gonna do?" he asked.

My pulse was racing. "I called him, yes, but I didn't text him," I said.

"Okay . . . "

"I'll know if his phone is on if a text goes through." I opened up Messages and sent him something brief.

Hey, where are you?

I hit SEND, watched the blue bubble sit, and sit, and . . . delivered!

"Ha!" I cheered, showing Pete the phone.

But Pete didn't quite share my enthusiasm. "So, his phone is on. How does that help us?"

I knew what to do. "One time," I said, feeling on top of the world, "in fall quarter, I *may* have gone to a frat party. I left my phone there—but I didn't realize until the next morning."

"Rough night," Pete said.

I soldiered on, trying not to even smile at his asides. "Anyway, I woke up, and I realized it wasn't there. So I found Maria, and we used this little app." I held up the phone for Pete to see, and pointed to the green radar scanner icon. "Find My iPhone. It was crazy easy. It dropped a little pin, and we followed it up to north campus, and dug my phone out of a bush under the fire escape. Boom."

Pete smiled, impressed. "All right, so let's go!"

I opened the app, but was immediately thrown off guard. Of course. We needed Dad's log-in information.

"Ugh!" I groaned. "We need his email and password."

Now it was Pete's turn to be confident. "I know two people who might be able to help."

– – –

We jogged down the stairs into the basement, to find Lily and Anna sprawled out on the carpet watching more *Doc McStuffins.* They still looked pretty wiped out after the long day.

"Hey, girls," I said. "Question for you."

They looked up at me, as if they had forgotten who I was. "What?" Lily asked.

"I need to get on your dad's Apple account," I said.

Anna raised an eyebrow. "Why? That's weird."

"He asked us to check something for him," Pete said quickly. "You guys don't know what his log-in info is, do you?"

Anna and Lily looked at each other. My fingers twitched in anticipation. Eventually Lily turned back to us. "We know the Netflix," she said, "and the Amazon and the Xfinity." Anna nodded solemnly, as if this was the most obvious thing in the world.

"Hmm," Pete said. "Do you know if he has a list of the passwords anywhere?"

The girls immediately nodded, and tore off ahead of us back upstairs. We sped after them. I wanted to hug them and tell them how they deserved so much better than this messed-up family situation they were in . . . but I decided to save that for later.

Anna was rooting around in a desk in the living room when we caught up to them. She pulled out tons of papers, tossing them on the floor. "Taxes . . . taxes . . . taxes . . . " she mumbled, bored. "Taxes" seemed to be a catchall term for everything adult. The papers looked more like coupons and thank-you notes but I said nothing.

Eventually, Anna pulled out a crisp piece of paper with a bunch of handwriting on it. "Here!" she cheered, presenting me with the information.

"You're perfect," I said, taking the paper.

"You are, too," Pete whispered to Lily, who was disgusted at Anna getting the only compliment.

I scanned the list. Anna had nailed it. There was his Apple log-in info, right in front of me.

Email: djackson@jackson-flowers.com

Password: saraj1018

My stomach lurched. *His password is my name and my birthday.* I fought off the pit in my stomach and turned back to the girls.

"Thank you guys so much," I said. "This is what we needed."

"Can we go watch TV now?" Lily whined.

"You bet," I said, and they took off. Pete and I sped back to the kitchen, where my phone sat, with the app open.

I entered his log-in information, and we watched the radar animation go around and around and around . . . until it stopped. There was the pin, at the corner of Alamo and Peterson, twenty minutes away.

"Well okay," Pete said. "At least it's not far."

I wasn't completely happy to see where he was. It was indisputable evidence that he'd lied to us today. He'd planned all along to go to this intersection, to whatever was there. Now I almost didn't want to know.

I didn't have to imagine too long. Pete had quickly pulled up an image of the intersection on Google Maps's street view. "Hey, take a look at this," he said. I peered over and looked at the 360-degree digital picture. The intersection was desolate. Two corners were abandoned lots, one corner featured a shabby Mexican restaurant, and the other was home to a small motel.

I looked up at Pete, my stomach churning. "Yuck."

"Yeah," he said softly. "This doesn't look good."

"But there's only one thing to do," I said. "I have to go."

"*We* have to go," Pete said. "I'm not letting you go over to that part of town alone. That's just asking for trouble."

"Thanks, but I'll be okay. Besides, we can't leave the girls alone here. And we *definitely* can't bring them with us."

Pete sighed, slowly nodding his head. "Sara, I'm really sorry about what I said before. I know the timing was terrible, I just had an impulse, and . . . "

I waved my hand. "Pete, this is terrible timing, too," I snapped. I got up, grabbed the car keys and headed to the door. But, my pulse racing, I turned back to face him. "I don't know what kind of game you're playing, but that's not how I roll. Wow—I thought you knew me better than this."

His face turned a dark red like I had never seen, raw emotion pouring out of his eyes and his trembling lips. He stood up to face me. "Sara, this is called friendship. I'm trying to be your best friend right now." His voice was shaking. "And if you don't like what you see, then that's your problem."

His words hit me like a ton of bricks, but instead of saying anything I turned and walked out the front door.

- - -

The intersection of Alamo and Peterson looked even worse in person than it did on the Internet. The sky had been taken over by low-hanging clouds as evening set in, which only made it look scarier and dirtier. There was *no one* around.

I parked the SUV in front of the Mexican restaurant, and got out. *Guadalajara: Just Like Grandma Made It!* the neon sign said, blinking on and off. I approached the front door and peered in the window. A high-school-age kid stood behind the counter, staring at nothing. There were no customers inside.

I groaned, realizing there was only one option left. *The motel it is.*

I jogged across the street towards the motel, which seemed to have no name whatsoever. I passed the front door of the lobby and turned into the small parking lot, and there it was: my little blue Corolla parked in front of room eight. The only car in the lot. I stood at the lip of the parking lot, breathing like a scuba diver about to go back down under. The idea of knocking on the door, on discovering Dad doing whatever he was doing . . . it all seemed like too much. Who was he in there with? What could he be up to? There was no way this would end well.

But my mind flashed back to the diner in Oklahoma. I remembered seeing the happy family in another booth, like they had walked straight out of a commercial. The two kids couldn't have known how lucky they were to have two parents on their side, in their corner.

In that moment, I was jealous, because those kids had something I wanted. And though I still felt jealous, I knew now I'd never have a happy couple of parents. I tried to force myself to accept that that kind of normalcy was never going to happen for me.

But at the same time, I still might be able to have *some* kind of father in my life, if I cared enough. Though he wasn't making it easy, I wasn't ready to give up on Danny Jackson.

And that's what moved my right foot forward onto the cracked asphalt of the parking lot. One foot in front of the other, I marched towards the door of room number eight. Right, left, right, left . . .

I knocked on the wooden door, softly at first. Nothing. I put my ear up toward the door and listened—for music, for the TV, for talking . . . nothing.

I knocked again, more forcefully this time—*rap, rap, rap!* I listened again. I heard a voice . . . was it Dad's? I couldn't tell what he was saying either. But I knocked again, harder than ever, now that I knew somebody was inside.

Suddenly I heard, "Ok*ay!* Ok*ay!*"

It was definitely Dad's voice, but the words were coming out of his mouth haltingly and bitterly.

He thrust open the door, and I immediately recoiled. The air coming out of the dark room reeked, a combination of sweat and alcohol and cigarettes. He was wearing a stained white undershirt and squinted in the light of the outside, such as it was.

I could barely look at him. I was so disgusted by the smell, by how he looked—by the entire scene.

"Sara?" he mumbled eventually. It sounded like his mouth was full of cotton balls.

"Yes," I said sternly.

Without saying anything else, he turned back into the room, taking his hand off the door. I slapped my hand onto the door and caught it before it latched closed. I threw it back open and marched inside. *You're not turning your back on me ever again.*

"Hey," I snapped. "What are you doing here?"

"Aw, Sara . . . " he moaned, flopping down on the bed. "I can't do it anymore. I just can't. It's all over."

"What are you—"

I was cut off by a big, earth-shattering sob. Dad

arched back and rolled on the bedspread like a colicky baby. His body thrashed and bent around as he cried.

I watched, unmoved. I wasn't going to comfort him. Not this time. My eyes searched the room, and I eventually pieced things together. There was a half-empty handle of gin, an empty carton of American Spirits. Two empty beer bottles stood next to another bottle lying on its side, a slow but steady stream of flat yellow beer dribbling onto the carpet.

"They're freaking out at your office," I said. "They have no idea where you are."

"I know, I know," he cried, burying his head under two flimsy pillows.

"So, what, you're just hiding out here, drinking?" I asked. He gave me no response. He just buried his head deeper. I tried again. "Why are you running away from everything?"

I'd had enough. I crossed to his bed and whipped the pillows away, tossing them against the wall. Flinging open the flimsy curtains, I yelled, "Hey! Answer my questions!"

Dad turned and looked at me, whimpering. We stared at each other like that for a while, neither of us moving a muscle.

"I don't deserve to be happy anymore," he said. "I lost you and your mother. I lost Teresa and the girls. I'm broken."

I wasn't sure what to say. He *had* broken off his first marriage and his second engagement. He *had* put all three of his daughters into jeopardy, even though Lily and Anna didn't know it yet.

But I still didn't think the Danny I had come to know over the last day, and the Danny I now saw before me, was a bad person. He had made plenty of mistakes, but he also wasn't the villain I thought he would be. And I knew I had a choice—to kick him while he was down, or to offer him a way up.

"You've screwed up. A lot. With me, with Mom, with Teresa, with the girls . . . " He groaned, thrashing around on the bed again. "But," I said sharply, "that doesn't mean you don't deserve to be happy."

He looked at me sharply, as if I had just thrown

cold water on him. "I'm trying to be patient, but I'm not gonna forgive you, if that's what you want me to say."

"I know that!" he screamed violently. It was a roar of pure rage, and for a minute I thought he might turn violent . . . until he rolled back over and quietly cried again.

Softly, almost to himself more than to me, he said, "I'm sorry." Then he said it again, and again, and more times than I could count. "You just met me," he said, "and this is how you're seeing me."

I sat down on the bed next to him. "I'm not scared of you, and I'm not running away from you. I'm still here . . . for some reason."

He looked at me—really looked at me—for the first time since I'd come in.

"All I know is that there are two girls at home who really want to see their dad," I said. I saw Dad's eyes fill up with tears, so I quickly added, "They're ready to forgive you, because they're young. But they won't wait around forever, either. They might not be as patient or as understanding as me, either."

Dad nodded slowly, like he was thinking about every word individually. Eventually he stopped, and I knew he'd heard me. "A new chapter starts now, Dad. Go take a shower," I said. "Then we can go home."

As he was sobering up in a hot shower, I sat in the dank, musty room. For whatever reason, Pete wandered into my mind. My stomach twisted into a big, fat knot at the thought of him. What was he doing at home right now? Sitting with the girls, trying to keep them happy as he wondered what had happened to their dad? What had happened to me?

I had to admit it to myself, I couldn't ask for a better friend than Pete. He volunteered to come on this trip, and though we never knew what was going to happen, the events of the last day were much more stressful and painful than we ever could have imagined. And yet he was still here, doing what he could to help me, Dad, and my sisters.

I heard my own voice in my head. *You've done a*

lot to push us away, but for whatever reason we're still around. I had just said that to Dad about me. Pete could just as easily say that *to me,* about *him.* I was doing nothing but pushing him away.

It was suddenly clear to me. If I kept pushing him away, I would lose my best friend, my support system, my confidante. Pete had never made my stomach flutter the way it did when Anthony Troy passed by on his longboard. But something told me Anthony Troy would never ride that longboard to the ends of the earth for me.

Before I could stare off into space any longer, Dad came out of the steamy bathroom dressed in his full suit again, looking much more like a businessman and father. "Okay," he said. "Let's go home."

– – –

The drive home was quiet. Both Dad and I had a lot on our minds. As we pulled into the driveway, I asked him one more question.

"Dad?" I asked. "How . . . often does this happen?"

"What?"

"How often do you pretend to be somewhere, when you're actually alone, and . . . "

He blushed and looked down at his hands, which were slightly trembling thanks to the chemicals still surging through his bloodstream. "I don't have a problem, if that's what you're asking."

I didn't believe him.

"Sara, please. I don't have a problem." He looked at me sternly, wearing the weight of the day on his weathered face. "Look . . . I'm really grateful you came to get me. And I'm so sorry you saw me like that. I want to do better. I'm going to do better. Okay?"

"That's easy to say," I said sternly. "If you're serious about doing better, I'm gonna hold you to it. And that starts by promising to never go off on benders in stupid, dirty motel rooms."

He nodded solemnly. "I know," he said. "You're right. I promise."

His words were devoid of emotion, but I turned off

the ignition, and he stepped out and bounded up the front stairs of the house, obviously putting on a happier face for the girls who waited inside.

"Honey, I'm home!" he bellowed brightly as he walked indoors.

"Daddy?" came a quiet call from the basement. Then I heard two sets of little feet pattering quickly up the carpeted stairs. Anna and Lily emerged, and bolted towards their father.

"Hey, sweeties!" Dad cheered, picking them both up at once. "I'm sorry I was gone so long. Sometimes you have to work extra hard to bring home the bacon, huh?" Hearing him lie so blatantly to his daughters made me sick. How long would he keep up this ruse with them? Had he gotten so used to lying that he wouldn't actually be able to turn the corner he promised me he would?

"Ooh, bacon!" Lily howled.

Anna giggled and said, "Bacon for dinner!"

"Did you have a good time with Sara and Pete?" Dad asked the girls.

"It was okay . . . ," Lily said. I braced myself. I knew what was coming.

Anna's smile faded. "They lost us."

"They what?" His voice was suddenly sharp.

"For only like half an hour," Lily offered. But the damage was done. I could tell Dad was shocked. Pete had emerged from the basement, and was watching this whole encounter with a look of pure dread.

Dad set the girls down on the floor. "Could you guys go get me a bottle of water from the fridge, please?"

The girls nodded and trotted off, unaware of the tension pulsing in the room.

"You didn't think it was worthwhile to tell me about that?" Dad spat.

"Funny you should say that," I fired back. "I tried calling you while we were looking for them—but you didn't answer your phone. And, wouldn't you know it, you weren't at your office either!" I walked right up to him and was inches away from his face when I said, "I wonder where you were."

I stepped backward, never losing eye contact. A long silence passed as we stared each other down. I willed myself not to think about Pete, standing there watching. I had a million things to say to him, too, but they would have to wait.

Eventually Dad sighed, and dropped his head. "You're right," he said. "I can't get mad at you for being irresponsible enough to lose track of those kids. I lost you for twelve whole years." He looked at me again, tears in his eyes. "I don't ever want to lose you again." His voice cracked and he rushed towards me, embracing me in a tight bear hug. I felt his heaving sobs against me, and I couldn't help but cry, too. I cried with relief for finally knowing my father. I cried for the hope that we might be able to care about each other and stay in each other's lives. I cried for the fact that in one day, I gained a father and two sisters, three things I never thought I'd have. And now that I'd come close to losing them, I realized all over again how much I needed them.

As we separated, I caught a glimpse of Pete out of

the corner of my eye. He stood awkwardly apart from us, trying to pretend he wasn't in the same room. "Sorry you had to see that, Pete," Dad said. "That you had to see all of this today. Really, I am."

Pete smiled tentatively. "That's okay, Mr. Jackson. I'm just glad everything is working out."

I turned to Dad. "Um, Dad, Pete and I are gonna take a walk. Cool? We'll be back soon." He nodded skeptically, but turned back and walked deeper into the house. I looked at Pete and inclined my head towards the front door.

Outside, I sat heavily on the stoop, unsure of how I was going to start this conversation. Pete sat down next to me, obviously unsure of where this was headed.

My eyes were still not dry from the relief of hugging Dad, and as soon as I started talking, they filled up again. "Pete," I started. "I am so, so sorry for the things I said earlier. For the way I've been acting since we came down here."

Before he could say anything, I kept going. "You need to know something. I just went and dug my dad out of a dirty motel room where he was hiding out all afternoon, drinking." Pete's eyes bugged out, but he said nothing. "I know. And while I was sitting in there waiting for him to get himself sober enough to walk out, I realized something. I realized that you came down here for me, and only me. Not for yourself. But for me. And I am beyond grateful for that."

Pete's face suddenly turned sour and he looked down. "Yeah, see? Do you hear what you just said?"

I was at a loss for words. My breath caught in my throat as I tried to respond, but Pete continued. "You're right. I came down here for you, and I've been working hard to support you this whole time, through thick and thin. But you don't owe me anything, okay? You don't have to be nice and say you love me, too." He stopped short, like the word *love* tasted rotten in his mouth.

My heart was pounding, and I couldn't tell if I was angry or hurt or panicked. Had I already broken his heart? Was this beyond fixing?

"If you're just trying to be nice, don't say anything,

okay? I already feel stupid for saying what I did, and I *really* don't want to get my hopes up all over again. So, I'm happy you're happy, but if it's okay with you, I think I'll head home. I'll catch a flight or something." He stood up and walked back inside.

I felt like I had just toppled off the end of the earth and was in total free fall. Pete had been the rock-solid foundation during one of the most chaotic weeks of my entire life. And just when I realized how much he meant to me, he disappeared. I knew I should leap up from the stoop, but my legs were heavy. My words had caused him nothing but pain. Maybe the best thing I could do was to shut up and let him walk away. My mind spinning and my stomach roiling, I lost track of time. The stars were peeking out in the sky, but I didn't let myself enjoy them. I didn't deserve to be happy after how much I had hurt someone who was guilty only of loving me.

Just then I heard the front door open behind me, and I turned, hoping to see Pete. But it was Lily and

Anna, looking like they had just received the worst news of their lives.

"Girls, what is it?" I asked, panicked.

"Pete is leaving," Anna said.

"Daddy is taking him to the airport," Lily said. "Why is he getting on an airplane? Are you leaving too?"

"Don't leave!" Anna begged.

"I'm . . . I'm not," I said. I realized, though, that part of me wanted to—even though leaving would mean saying goodbye to Lily, Anna, and Dad. But in this moment nothing was more important than staying with Pete.

"Hold on," I said, finally standing up. "Wait a second, girls." I brushed past them back into the house. Dad stood in the entryway looking concerned.

"What happened? Pete just sped in here and told me he needs a ride to the airport. He opened his phone and booked a plane ticket in about five minutes. I'll call him an Uber as soon as he's ready. He said his flight leaves in ninety minutes. Is he okay?"

My heart rate kicked up a hundred notches. "Where is he?"

"Packing his bag," Dad said. "Upstairs."

I dashed up the long staircase, beads of sweat popping up on my neck. I burst into the guest room to find Pete scowling and throwing his clothes into his suitcase. "Pete," I said, "stop. Wait."

"I already booked a ticket, Sara," he said. Hearing him say my name killed me. Tears escaped my eyes and I was immediately short of breath.

"Let me just say one more thing, then. Before you leave." He turned to look at me, though he kept balling up T-shirts and burying them in his suitcase. "You're right, I *do* owe you." Immediately I knew that was the wrong thing to start with. He rolled his eyes bitterly and looked away again.

"But wait! Wait!" I yelled desperately. "That is not *why* I love you." He stopped suddenly like I had shot an arrow into his back. "I know I love you because without you here, this trip wouldn't have been half of what it was. Having you here meant I could watch you charm my dad even while I held back. I got to watch you become inseparable with those girls. I mean, I wouldn't have even *gotten* here without you. I drove up to this house on the first night laughing and happy—not scared, not ready to turn around—because being with you gives me strength. Pete, you made this trip what it was. You make my life what it is. I never, ever want to go back to what my life was like before."

Finally, Pete looked up and met my eyes. He put a hand in front of his mouth as he inhaled ragged breaths, his eyes red with tears. "Sara," he said. He smiled, and opened his arms wide. "Then you got me. I'm here."

I sprinted across the room and wrapped my arms around him tight. I could have stayed there forever. The room was silent except for our heaving breaths. I pulled my head off his chest and grabbed his face with both hands. I kissed him hard, our lips interlocking like they had been made for each other.

Eventually I pulled my face away a few inches and

looked into his sweet, green eyes. "I've wanted to do that for a long time," Pete said. "I have to admit."

I laughed bashfully. "As good as you hoped?"

He smiled. "I think we'll get there."

− − −

Three days later, it was time for Pete and me to make the drive back home. After the first day that felt like an eternity, the rest of the trip flew by. We had taken trips around Dallas, visited Dad's office, cooked gourmet meals in the beautiful kitchen, and stayed up until the wee hours of the morning talking.

Lily, Anna, and I left Pete at home and spent a whole afternoon together, just the three of us. They introduced me to their American Girl dolls, Samantha and Lea, and the three of us went on tons of adventures together, real-life trips to the zoo and the movies, and imaginary trips to Japan and Mars.

But somehow the three days came to an end, and Pete and I found ourselves loading our bags into the

Corolla under another stunning Texas morning sun. "When will you be back?" Anna demanded, her tiny body wrapped around my right leg.

"Sometime soon, I promise," I said. "But we're gonna FaceTime every week. You're gonna get sick of me—that's how much you're gonna see of me."

Both girls rolled their eyes. "You'll never get sick of me, though, right?" Pete chimed in. The girls shook their heads and chuckled. "You just love me for my red hair!" Pete cried.

I walked over to Dad, who was admiring the scene from the front steps. "Well," I said, "I guess this is goodbye. For now."

"Not too long, though," he said.

"What do I tell Mom?" I asked.

Dad grimaced. "You tell her whatever you want, Sara. I want to do anything I can to patch things up with her, too, if she's ready for that."

"I don't know," I said. "This is going to take a lot of work."

He nodded. "I know that. And I don't expect either

of you to ever completely forgive me. I just hope you believe me when I say I want to be a part of your life, and of hers. If you'll have me."

"I can't speak for Mom, but I believe in you, Dad."

He smiled sweetly, and embraced me. "Then there's no use drawing this out any longer. You guys better get going while you have some daylight left."

I nodded, squeezing him one last time. Pete came over and shook Dad's hand—with their secret handshake they had made up. Pete put his arm around my waist as we said one final goodbye and walked back down towards the car.

– – –

When we reached the Oklahoma border, it was dusk. Over the course of the afternoon, low-hanging clouds had rolled in above, casting the world in blue and gray. All of a sudden, the sky opened up, and sheets of rain pounded the highway and the roof of the car.

"Yikes!" Pete cried from behind the wheel. We couldn't see more than a few inches ahead of us.

"Pull over! Pull over!" I cried. Pete angled the car onto the shoulder and put it in park.

"Man, I hope this doesn't last long," Pete said, putting the hazard lights on and sitting back.

"Where else do we have to go?" I said, smiling. I leaned over and kissed him. He held my face in his hands and tenderly stroked my cheek with his thumb, like an arrowhead skimming the surface of a lake.

Under the incessant clatter of rain on the roof, it was just us. The space inside my little powder blue car might have been the whole world.